# FIVE FROM THE BORDERLANDS

# Other CV-2 Books by Raymund Eich

### Stone Chalmers
The Progress of Mankind
The Greater Glory of God
To All High Emprise Consecrated
In Public Convocation Assembled

### The Confederated Worlds
Take the Shilling
Operation Iago
A Bodyguard of Lies

### Novels
The Blank Slate
New California
The Reincarnation Run

### Short Novels
The ALECS Quartet
A Mighty Fortress

# FIVE FROM THE BORDERLANDS

## *Raymund Eich*

CV-2 Books • Houston

# LA RUBIA

The house looked like home. Four stucco walls ringed the courtyard. The sky was the same deep blue as the sky over the hills above Guadalajara. But this sky was the inside of a dome barely larger than the house, papered over with an array of light-emitting fluorophores. A fountain gently shot water drops in arcs that took ten minutes to land. At its best, her house gave Francisca pleasant dreams of flying through the original back on Earth, with her husband and her children nearby; but at times it only reminded her of all she had lost.

Francisca floated a few meters from the gate. Mist from the fountain had condensed on her strap-on plastic wings. Next to her hovered her assistant, José, and her daughter, Annamaria.

"They're crossing the plaza," José said. "They'll be here in—"

"I have eyes in my head." Francisca glared at José. His obsolete interface looked like pale warts—three around each eyesocket, one on each ear, one under his nose—on his broad bronzed Indio face. Over his shoulder, in her mind's eye, she saw Mauricio, her other assistant, lead the European and his killer arēs to the mouth of her corridor.

"I'm sorry, Señora," José said.

— Mama,—came Annamaria's voice direct to her brain.—Don't be so harsh with him.—

Her daughter was only sixteen; too young to remember how accursedly lazy the lower orders could be. But Francisca was young enough to remember her own teenage idealism during the 2020s boom, an idealism that chafed at the weary cynicism of her parents. Annamaria would learn soon enough. — My nerves are on edge, — Francisca said.

— I know. But Mauricio and José are right. It's become too dangerous. You know that, Mama. We need protection. —

— But a European! His arēs may have killed your brother! —

Annamaria rolled her eyes. Why did her brother's memory mean so little? A chime rang from outside the courtyard and brought Francisca's attention around. She looked through the gate. Mauricio drifted with his foot hooked in a rayon loop on the corridor floor. The European and his arēs wore zero-gee jetvests.

Mother of God, she wished it hadn't come to this. With time, José could have rigged more weapons, and the next pirate ship raiding for iron and nickel would have been blown apart. But the European's arēs carried the blueprints for better weapons in er soulless machine brain. A quarter-million euros for three months of arming and training might turn out to be money well spent on hiring the two.

"Señora," José said. "Should we admit them?"

Francisca nodded. — Open, — she told the gate. Its halves folded in. Mauricio withdrew his foot from the loop, and flapped in like an overfed bird. This was the first time she'd seen the other two in person. The European — his name was Dietrich; she might as well refer to him by it — stood about one-meter-sixty-five. Was he short, or had he neglected his bone density while living in the asteroid belt? Dietrich had a wiry figure, ragged blond hair, and a scar over his left eye. A laser pistol sat holstered on his hip. He reminded Francisca of venal policemen back home in Mexico; tell them you knew the state governor, or someone high up in Mexico City, and they would slink away.

The arēs looked like a child's mannequin with stubby wings on er back. E had eyes, ears, nose, mouth; and a collection of levers underneath er beige polymer skin to distort er face in mimicry of emotions. Francisca had seen civilian intelligent robots, commonly known as athenas, once or twice, but never before an arēs, an intelligent robot whose neural network brain had been selected for military use. E should look evil, monstrous, or at the very least, aged beyond er years by er time in combat. Instead e looked like a well-behaved child.

Mauricio stopped his flight with careful flaps. Dietrich and his arēs puffed air from their vests' front vents into the faces of Fransica and the others. Mauricio cleared his throat. "Señora Jünger, may I introduce Major Dietrich, formerly of the European Rapid Response Force?"

He glanced at her hand. She didn't lift it. He bowed. "At your service, Señora." He spoke lisping Continental Spanish, probably through a translation computer wired into his ears and voice. "And at that of your sister." Dietrich began to bow at Annamaria, but instead she held out her hand, palm down. He bent and kissed it.

Flattering unction. "My daughter, Annamaria."

"Daughter? I would never have guessed. You look so alike, both your hair is so white-blonde—"

"Some Mexicans are of pure European descent," Francisca said. Her people called her *la rubia*, the blonde, and had called her that for the decade since she'd gathered them in the ruins of Mexico and led them to the Brazilian space elevator and a new life in the asteroid belt. They called Annamaria *la rubicita*, and the respect they gave Francisca they transferred to her daughter. No one needed to know she'd tinted Annamaria's hair with gene-therapy colorizer when her daughter was two years old.

"Pardon me," Dietrich said. "Señora, Señorita, may I introduce Marlborough?"

The arēs bowed to Francisca, then Annamaria. E opened er mouth, and words came from a speaker where er tongue should be. "I am honored to meet you," e said with a sexless tenor voice.

Francisca didn't look at er. "Why is it speaking to me?"

Dietrich lifted his chin. "Marlborough is my subordinate. E is not my pet. E speaks for erself."

"Perhaps Señora Jünger is discomfited by the EU's invasion of Mexico during the North Atlantic War," Malborough said to Dietrich.

Shut up.

"You have told her? About our deployment to Mexico from August 2047 through May 20—"

"Shut up!" Francisca shouted. "If I want you to speak I'll ask!" For this thing to be moving, talking, pretending to be alive while her son was dead, perhaps even at this machine's hand—!

"Your pardons, Señora," Marlborough said. Er vest puffed and e drifted a few dozen centimeters back.

Francisca glared at Dietrich, while rapid breaths flared out her narrow nose. He avoided her gaze and cast a sidelong glance at his arēs. "Tell us about your deployment to Mexico, Major," she said.

Dietrich blinked and bobbed his head. "Yes, well, we had our orders, and it was better for the world we opened a second front on the Americans and brought the war to a close more quickly...."

Francisca returned her gaze to the arēs. At least e seemed willing to talk. "Tell me."

"I directed a battery of robotic rocket artillery. We landed at Tampico, and moved west to Ciudad Valles, San Luis Potosi, Lagos de Moreno, and Guadalajara…. Señora?"

Her estate had lain along the road from Lagos de Moreno. During the army's retreat, Oskar, her son, drove up to the house and told them to shelter in the basement. Why had they listened? They should have fled with him. They should have shared his fate.

"Señora," Marlborough said, "I regret any damage to your property and any physical or emotional pain my actions may have caused you and those close to you." E sounded sincere, and er face drooped in contrition.

Francisca shut her eyes. Who was this damned machine to pity her with er neural network emotions?

Dietrich cleared his throat. "I think we'd do better to leave the past in the past. Now, as we had discussed, over the next three months we will arm your settlement and train your citizens—"

"No. No! We don't need you, we don't need your killer arēs. Get out!"

"Señora?" said José.

— Mama, what are you doing?—

— They destroyed our farm! Our country! We can't work with them!—

"We had agreed," Dietrich said. "The terms are fair."

"That's before we knew what you had done to us." Francisca

folded her arms.

— To you and I, Mama. — Annamaria leaned forward. "Señor, would the two of you please wait outside?"

Dietrich opened his mouth to protest, but his expression showed he thought better of it. "Gladly, Señorita." He and Marlborough rotated toward each other, then flew toward the gate.

Francisca turned her back on the European with a few flaps of her wings. She sent her next words not just to Annamaria's brain, but also to José and Mauricio's earbud speakers. — Everyone lost something to the Europeans, if not to that one and his arēs. It's beneath our dignity to accept their offer. — Across the courtyard, the gate's halves folded shut. One hinge crackled. A camera showed Dietrich and the machine in the corridor, heads together, doubtless speaking mind-to-mind.

Mauricio turned his head and breathed heavily, and José's mouth puckered. "You don't agree," Francisca said.

Mauricio exhaled sharply, then looked up. "We lost everything once. If we don't learn from Dietrich how to defend ourselves, we'll lose everything again."

"Some pirates will want more than the refined metal in the warehouse," José said. "We couldn't stop someone from conquering us. We need him and his arēs."

"José," Francisca said gently, "they killed your wife. How can you overlook that?"

He narrowed his eyes. "The Aztecs ate the heart of Doña Malinche's brother, but she still should have taken their side against Cortes. We have greater enemies than that man."

"It's only three months," Mauricio added. "Only a quarter-million euros. If the new platinum vein we found is as pure and extensive as it seems, that quarter-million will be only a few percent of our income."

"If we'll have so much money we can hire a defense consultant who isn't European. There must be Americans in the belt providing the same service."

José nodded sadly. "If we can find one, and sell enough platinum to pay him, before the next pirate raid. We shouldn't risk so much."

Mauricio cleared his throat. "I've never heard of any Americans with their own arēs, either."

Francisca lifted her gaze to meet her daughter's. If Annamaria took her side, the two men would yield. "What do you think?"

She raised her wings in a gesture encompassing the two men. "I agree with them."

"But that machine killed your brother—"

"—who was a saint among men and the flower of Mexican manhood! By the Virgin! The government failed! It gave Oskar scared men with old rifles and told him to stop a horde of war machines remote-controlled by a mind a thousand times faster than his! Think of the living, Mama."

The weight of the consensus against Francisca sunk in. They wanted Dietrich and his arēs. They'd rather sleep easier than maintain their dignity. "Very well. We'll hire them. But no one mentions the new platinum vein to them, and we hide its operations as best we can."

Dietrich and Marlborough started well. They slept and Dietrich took meals on their ship, but they worked twelve-hour days among the asteroid's people. The first week, the arēs labored in the settlement's assemblery, floating at vat number four's control panel with a data cable plugged into a socket on er chest. Once Marlborough copied er instruction files into the vat's volatile memory, the vat's hundred-quadrillion carbon nanotube fingers did the rest. They pulled atoms from storage, moved them into place, and used heat and electron flows to add them to the growing structures. Infrared scopes and radars to better see pirates coming. Missiles and gamma-ray lasers to cripple pirate ships before they docked. Demo charges, shrapnel mines, and genomically-tailored paralytic gas, against pirates who did dock. Hardened and wireless communication links, triply redundant, to put their defenses together.

Francisca hosted a dinner on Thursdays for Mauricio, José, and the settlement's other leaders, to discuss events. This week, they drifted in the courtyard among squeezebulb martinis, sushi assembled in rice-paper wraps, and the sounds of twelve-tone pieces by Schoenberg. Her people needed their cultural horizons broadened beyond tortillas and mezcal.

"Señora," José said, "we should hack vat four when the arēs uses it, and copy the files for the weapons."

Mauricio's eyes widened. "Fool! They'll stop building them if we try."

"If they find out. If we're lucky, they won't."

Francisca's eyebrows rose in pleasant surprise at José's idea. "Would it matter so much if they stopped building weapons? They've already assembled many."

"No." Annamaria flung an empty squeezebulb at a trashbird robot. The trashbird craned its neck but missed, and the bulb sailed past the fountain. "They've tamper-proofed the weapons they've already assembled. They'll all melt if we try reverse-engineering even one of them."

"So, *rubicita*?" José asked.

"They're smart enough to do the same thing if we try stealing the weapon instruction files. If we try to cheat them, they'll punish us. I've talked to Dietrich a bit, and that's the sense I have of him."

Francisca frowned, but nodded. Information wasn't power. *Proprietary* information was power. Of course Dietrich and the arēs knew that; they came from a culture that dominated Earth by keeping its most important secrets.

*A bit*? How many times had Annamaria spoken with the European? Francisca checked her daughter's movements a few times after that, but her visits with Dietrich were brief and took place in public during the asteroid's day.

As Marlborough assembled the sensors and weapons, Dietrich emplaced them. Francisca went along once, with a spray canister of vacuumset on her back, to see what it required. Two trashbirds clutched a gamma-ray laser in their claws, one by the barrel and the other by the capacitor slot. José flew awkwardly with pieces of the laser's mounting brace slung over his chest, and when the trashbirds ignored his shouted commands he used his interface to jolt the robots' neural nets with pleasure or pain. Children flew after them, or darted from handhold to handhold along the walls, until they reached the active mineheads and José warned the children away. Dietrich jetted slowly, unreeling data and power lines; one of his mindless robots, the size of a bat, slithered along the cables, licked adhesive over them, and wrestled them to the wall. They went up a narrow corridor off the active nickel minehead, where they suited up, went out a new airlock, and tethered themselves. They floated at the bottom of a hole three meters wide and five deep. The sun hung over them, small and dim but brighter than any other of the many stars, and Francisca realized she hadn't seen the sun in years. Soon, the hole's rim clipped the sun, and shortly after, shadow filled the entire hole.

The men spent three hours mounting the laser, charging the capacitors, and topping off the lasing dye. The asteroid had just rotated them back into sunlight when Dietrich tested the laser on a rock Marlborough had put into orbit two hundred meters away. Three bursts of the laser started the rock melting and spewing vapor. Francisca handed José the vacuumset canister, and he sprayed shut the hole.

After the equipment had been assembled and emplaced, Dietrich and Marlborough set up a training schedule. Dietrich drilled everyone—men, women, older teenagers—on scrambling out to the lasers and firing them manually. Marlborough trained people to operate the lasers from the command computers distributed through the settlement, and worked to set up everyone's interfaces to allow firing by thought.

For three weeks, Francisca found excuses to avoid training under Marlborough. Two teenage boys had a fistfight, and she had to call in the boys, their parents, and the girl of whom both boys were enamored; an encrypted message came in from one of their metals buyers, he'd be drifting by in a few weeks; she had a new household robot assembled and had to train it… she couldn't hide the truth from herself any longer. Her hatred of Marlborough was why she avoided training. She turned back to her new robot, and when it put her underwear in her sock bag she jolted its pain center with a glee which quickly shamed her. "There, there," she said, as the robot clung to her ankle and she, through her interface, sent it a mild but long wave of pleasure.

Francisca woke that night around two. She'd soaked her sleeping bag's lining with sweat, in some bad dream that faded when she woke. She looked around the room, in the hope that some new angle would remind her what her dream had been; but all she saw was the courtyard lit by the false stars in the ceiling. Her household robots shuffled on their perch, nervous over something. She thought of the shocks she'd given the new one, and wondered if it had bad dreams as well.

After a few minutes, she realized she wouldn't fall back asleep. She crawled out of her sleeping bag—the sweat on her skin chilled her—and jumped to her wardrobe. She pulled on a long-sleeved shirt, cargo pants, and her wings, and went through the courtyard and into the dim corridor. Dietrich had installed a new gun emplacement a few hundred meters away across the asteroid; if she couldn't sleep, she could at least be productive and take a look.

On her return she flapped carefully, winding through a section where the corridor had followed a twisting nickel vein and mineheads gaped in the darkness. The platinum vein, so pure it was almost as blond as her hair, lay down one of them. She flew on, and as she rounded one corner, Marlborough said, "Señora?"

She twisted around and lifted her knees toward her torso. "Mother of God!" She flapped to stabilize herself, but ended up spinning.

Marlborough jetted a puff of air from er suit, gripped her wrist, and stopped their motion. "My apologies." E spoke an upper-class Mexico City Spanish dialect. Er skin was cold and too smooth.

"What do you want?" Francisca asked.

"I would like to speak with you, if I may."

"I'm sorry I haven't attended any of your training sessions yet, but I've been busy."

Marlborough shook er head. "I understand. However, I sought you to speak of another matter."

How had e known she was here? Was e spying on her? Worse, was e spying on their platinum mining operation? "I don't want to talk now. I'm tired."

"Judging by your heartrate and breathing, you are unlikely to fall asleep. However, I understand if now is not a good time."

Why did e want to talk? Oskar? Did e know more about his fate? She buried the thought. She refused to lose her dignity by letting this machine see her hope. Francisca straightened and glared at Marlborough. "Tell me what you have to tell, and then I'm going to bed."

"Thank you, Señora." E shut er mouth for a second. "Before you, I had never met someone whom my service to Europe had harmed."

Anger bloomed in Francisca, like a fire when a log rolled. Her gaze pored over the arēs' face in search of a reason to stifle her rage, but found none on the smooth bland plastic. "You want me to unburden your guilt? To forgive you for destroying my livelihood and killing my son? I don't know what your emotions are, but if you feel something like guilt I want you to be stained with it forever."

Marlborough widened er brown eyes, but er tenor voice remained even. "I appreciate your candor, Señora. However, I do not expect your forgiveness. I only wish to clarify my motivations, and those of the other arēs who participated in the invasion of Mexico."

"Whether you viewed us with hatred or contempt? Do you think I want to know the answer?"

"We weren't bred to look down on Mexicans, or non-Europeans in general. We were bred to serve our European masters, and bred in how to serve: to direct fire and movement, advance and retreat, for hundreds of robots; to work with our peers and our superiors; to be brave and efficient; to feel joy in our service."

Francisca sniffed out a breath. "It was in your *nature* to destroy Mexico. That's an even better defense than following orders. A higher level of moral absolution." She shut her eyes, and the moment she learned of Oskar's death came back to her. The survivor services officer hadn't yet left the house. Fernando's strong arms protected her while she cried, and his baritone voice murmured. War throws dice to claim its victims. She squeezed her eyes shut harder. She would not show this machine her tears.

"I do not seek moral absolution," Marlborough said. "I do not deny my responsibility for the suffering I caused."

Her eyes snapped open. "Then what do you want from me?"

"I want you to know that, for the first time in my existence, I feel guilt for treating someone other than my masters improperly. It is not pleasant, but it is what I feel and what I deserve, and I do not doubt I will be stained with it forever."

Francisca clenched her fists. The damned arēs and er imperturbable airs. Would it be worse if e had no guilt, or if e had nothing but? An attack came to mind, and she used it. "Your guilt is why your masters discarded you."

"Señora?" Er tone showed er weakness.

"What good is an arēs that feels qualms about its job? You failed the evolutionary fitness test, didn't you? None of Europe's new arēs have brains modelled on your brain, do they?" The aress were bred to serve. Although they were born in an assemblery vat instead of a stall at a stud farm, the same principle applied. Only the ones whose traits most pleased humans would be the parents of the next generation.

Marlborough nodded. "Señora, true, my masters studied my performance, and decided my brain was not suitable as a template for future offspring."

Francisca leaned forward, and her facial muscles were firm. "How does it feel to know you're sterile?" Like an intelligent steer? No, like an intelligent bull with no access to cows.

Marlborough blinked twice. "I want to be reproduced, yes. I was very disappointed when the ERRF declined to reproduce me. But Dietrich has told me that someday it will happen, if I continue my good work for him."

"So you'll have offspring someday? arēs sharing most of your mental traits?"

"Yes. Dietrich told me so."

Francisca's chest swelled with a deep breath. "If you do, I hope you see them die." She turned and flapped her wings for home. The arēs could have caught her with er jetvest, and she expected er to do so. When e didn't, she smiled a gloating smile. She'd shown er who was master.

She soon reached the settlement's central plaza, a nearly cubic room about twenty meters on a side. A few meters to the left was the mouth of the corridor leading home. The other main residential corridor emerged on the plaza's opposite face, and the mouth of the corridor leading to the warehouse and the docking facility was on the face that could, just barely in the asteroid's faint gravity, be defined as up. A few other doors lead from the plaza to the assemblery, the infirmary, the chapel, the bone density maintenance lab, and other public spaces. No one was about at this hour, and only a few dim lights glowed. She turned to her corridor, and had gone a few meters in when she heard a couple's voices from the service corridor.

Was that Annamaria? But her daughter was home in bed; so Francisca's interface said. And Dietrich? Francisca spun around, and flapped quietly to the corridor mouth. She took a handhold along the upper wall and peered around the corner at the couple.

Annamaria's hair looked white in the pale light, and the lean arms and puffing jetsuit indicated Dietrich floated next to her. "Why do I have to be so quiet?" he asked, louder than before but with a playing-along tone.

"Because there are only 300 people on this rock," Annamaria said quietly. "Because the one time I let a local boy run his hand up my shirt, Mama glared at me for a month."

Dietrich lowered his voice. "She thinks you're—"

"A virgin? What she doesn't know won't hurt her."

*Of course* Francisca had suspected. At least, if she was speaking truthfully, Annamaria had only been with visitors—the son of the travelling American physician, Tung, probably, or maybe the smooth-faced Australian nickel hauler. Francisca remembered her own teenage years, thinking she'd hidden her own adventures from her mother's eyes. The memory didn't make it any more pleasant to hear, though. Then Annamaria spoke again. "Sorry?"

"I said, so you weren't?"

"Wasn't it obvious?"

"Well, that, yes," Dietrich said.

Annamaria's voice grew more firm. "Is that a problem?"

"No. Of course not. You're a healthy teenage girl doing what's natural."

Annamaria said nothing for a moment, then leaned over and kissed him. "I need to get home, and fix my hack of the house's security before I go to bed." They kissed again, several times, their lips wet. Francisca pushed off her handhold back down the corridor. Her own daughter, with the monster's master?

A few seconds later, Annamaria swooped into the corridor. She hunched her shoulders. "Mama, what are you doing awake?"

They were in public. Someone might hear them. "We will discuss it at home," Francisca said, her tone pinched and cool. She wanted her daughter to know she'd been caught.

Annamaria lifted her chin. "No, let's discuss it here."

"This is a public space."

"If you know, there's no one else I need to keep it secret from."

Francisca covered her mouth with her clenched fist. "How many times?"

"With Dietrich?" Annamaria shrugged. "Five or six."

"Why?"

"Why? Because he's a man. He's not like the boys from here, or even the young travelers. He's seen so much. Much more than you. He was born in Leipzig. He's seen Berlin and Paris. The ruins of Delhi and Moscow. Every major settlement in the asteroid belt. He's sophisticated and wise."

Francisca laughed coldly. "Do you think you mean anything to him? When he's done he'll take his pay to the brothels near the Ceres spaceport—"

"Do you think I'm a little girl playing Barbie and Ken?" Annamaria's face was red. "I've had enough of boys who think a hidden tryst means love. Dietrich's too mature to believe in that."

"Too old."

Annamaria smirked. "Old enough to be my brother."

Francisca's open palm slapped hard against her daughter's cheek. "You will not mock his memory!"

One door, then another, creaked open along the corridor. Annamaria kept her gaze on her mother, and absently rubbed her cheek. "Go home to your ghost son and your ghost husband and leave me alone."

"Where do you think you're going?"

"To Dietrich. He doesn't have to take me very far; just off this damn rock."

"You're not old enough to leave," Francisca said. Annamaria flapped backward. "You're not!"

"The way you treat me, I'm too old to stay!" Annamaria rolled over and flapped vigorously into the plaza and out of sight.

Francisca went home, but seethed too much to sleep.

The next few days, she heard whispers throughout the settlement, but no one would meet her eye. Annamaria ate and slept in Dietrich's ship. Francisca wondered how her anger at the European would manifest itself when she saw him, but she never did. He must have been tracking her movements and avoiding her.

She could contact him, or Annamaria, or both, through the interface if she wanted to. It wouldn't do any good. The only reason to talk to Annamaria would be to vent her anger at her daughter. Venting might feel pleasant, but it would only drive Annamaria further into Dietrich's arms.

A few mornings later, Marlborough called. E appeared from the shoulders up in a window overlaid on Francisca's vision. A training session on the new armaments and sensors in a half hour, could she attend?

Go to the devil, she wanted to say, but the arēs looked and spoke submissively. Cursing er would be like jolting her robots for no reason. Besides, she had to attend sometime for the sake of her people.

The training took place in the chapel. Instead of pews, the sanctuary had a half-dozen nets stretching wall-to-wall and floor-to-ceiling. Instead of looking to the altar and Christ in his agony above it, though, people clipped their belts to the rearmost net and faced the back wall. Locals of all ages, from teenagers to José's ancient father-in-law, Esteban, hung on the net, and interfaced with anything from handheld computers to skin-mounted buds. Francisca was the only one with circuits linked directly to her neurons, but she knew some people planned to upgrade the next time Dr. Tung passed through.

Marlborough set them to drills, and er attention jumped among them like a chess master playing a dozen opponents at once. Francisca closed down her local senses almost entirely, and for a few moments felt like she'd become her asteroid, its sensors become her eyes as a simulated pirate ship approached, its hydraulics and servos become her muscles as she limbered and fired her weapons. She pitied those pressing buttons, or watching ghostly graphics flashed on their retinas.

After three hours, the session broke up. Francisca turned her head to unclip herself when air swished nearby. She looked up and met the arēs' gaze.

"Señora, may I have a moment?"

"What about?"

E looked about, and spoke softly. "Major Dietrich knows about the high purity platinum vein."

Francisca's fingers clenched around strands of netting and her clip. The arēs twisted the knife further. "God damn you."

"I'm sorry?"

"God damn you for telling him."

"No! Señora. I have known about it for weeks, but I haven't passed the information to him."

"For weeks." Had the settlement kept any secrets from this machine? From Dietrich? Did the European know everything about their business save what the arēs had chosen not to tell?

"I determined it from data gathered throughout the asteroid. I saw robots haul ore from an interior tunnel at times when Dietrich was aboard our ship, followed by smelter runs at temperatures suitable for platinum vaporization. Also, I detected five tons of platinum in your warehouse, hidden underneath iron and nickel ingots."

*We're poor settlers, without a legal basis for our claim. A quarter-million euros is all we can afford.* How angry had Dietrich become when he had discovered she'd lied? "I'm to believe you didn't tell your master?"

"We signed a contract to equip and train you for defense. Our task does not involve prying into your community's affairs. Your daughter told him. She suggested to him we steal it when we depart."

Francisca shut her eyes. This couldn't be Annamaria's plan. Turning against the settlement was bad enough, but to consider such a blow against her mother! "That damned whore," she said, voice tight.

"I'm sorry," Marlborough said, and the platitude and er flat voice refocused Francisca's anger.

"Sorry? Why have you told me this?"

"You deserve to know."

"Know they're going to steal from me? How can I stop them?" She grabbed the arēs's shoulder. "Are you offering to help me?"

"Help you?"

"Hide the platinum. Increase security in the warehouse." Marlborough kept er gaze on her eyes, but er head bobbed. "Persuade them not to do it. Would you even do that?"

E looked down. "I'm sorry, I can't."

Francisca pushed the arēs, but e stopped er motion and spin with vest puffs. "Don't you dare say *can't* when you mean *won't*! Fucking machine!"

Marlborough raised er palms. "Señora, no, it lies beyond my power. I'm not choosing Dietrich on a rational basis. I'm compelled to side with him."

She kicked the arēs's abdomen, aiming for er brain. "Compelled? It's the way your neural network is more likely to fire, nothing more! Get out of my sight!" Text appeared in her vision. She'd severely bruised her toe on Marlborough's braincase. An infirmary visit was indicated.

Marlborough bowed er head and jetted out of the chapel. Francisca watched er leave, then decided to experience the pain from her toe. Her foot throbbed, and she winced until she turned the pain off. She flew across the plaza to the infirmary. The plaza's ceiling showed a noontime summer sky puffed with a few clouds. After drinking a vial of microrobots programmed to speed healing of her bruise, she went home for the rest of the day to drink martinis and fume about her daughter. A somber mood hung over the weekly dinner gathering that night.

The next afternoon, Francisca chaired a meeting of the mining managers when she realized Dietrich wanted to talk. She frowned, and almost refused, until he leaked conciliation to her. Fine. "Pardon me," she said to the men around her, and shifted most of her attention to the European.

Her interface made the room seem dim and quiet. The miners became gray figures with soft, muffled speech. The only bright spot was a window in her vision, showing Dietrich from somewhere in his ship. He'd grown a thin blond goatee, and Francisca felt glad her interface had shunted her emotions away from her body's muscles and into her manifestation to the European. "What do you want?"

Dietrich smiled ruefully. "Marlborough told me e talked to you. I want to apologize. I'm not going to do what you think I am."

"I'll believe that when you're gone and the platinum's still here."

"We'd like to reconcile with—"

"Don't you dare speak for me."

Dietrich blinked a few times. "Annamaria and I. We'd like to speak to you in person and make things clear. Perhaps tonight?"

"Perhaps not."

"Then tomorrow, or the next day. We'll keep asking until you agree."

Francisca sniffed out a virtual breath. "Fine. Tonight, eight o'clock, my house."

"Thank you, Señora. We'll see you then."

She quickly cut the connection. The miners looked up when she returned to her body. Figuratively, though, half her mind remained absent from the meeting, and the rest of her duties that day. Dietrich and her daughter weren't coming to negotiate; they would announce Annamaria would leave with him. Perhaps they would leave the platinum, but the platinum didn't matter, not as much as her daughter. Sixteen was a dangerous age: old enough to feel like an adult, but too young to think like one. Dietrich would abandon her in the grimy port district of a big asteroid, Ceres or Pallas. She would never see her daughter again. The pain of losing one child had almost broken her. She had to make Annamaria see the suffering she'd cause her mother, if she lost the other.

They arrived at her house precisely at eight. Francisca made them wait a few seconds before she opened the gate. Dietrich flew in the middle of their line, with Annamaria on his right and Marlborough on his left. Under the European's eyes lay purple bags, and he tapped his fingers on his thigh. Annamaria kept her cold-eyed gaze on the cobblestones and flowerbeds. The arēs had a placid, hopeful expression. *Yes, let Dietrich and I part happily, and Christ will wash all your guilt away.* Francisca glared a moment at the arēs, until e saw her and er smile faded.

They stopped a few meters from Francisca. Dietrich bowed. "Señora."

"Welcome," she said, in a tone that didn't mean it. She would be a civil hostess, but no more. "Wine?"

"Thank you," Dietrich said. Through the interface, Francisca called a small robot. It jumped from shoulder to shoulder and tossed squeeze-bulbs of pinot grigio into their hands. Marlborough frowned at ers. Dietrich lifted his bulb, but didn't drink.

"Say what you have to say." Francisca kept her voice even.

He smiled, sipped wine, smiled again. "I know you're angry. You think I'm going to abduct your daughter—"

"She thinks she's an adult, so I'll grant her that. She's going of her own choice. Foolish though it is."

"It's better than living in my dead brother's shadow," Annamaria said.

Dietrich raised his hand and shook his head. "She's not leaving."

"What? You said you'd get me out of here!"

He smiled at Annamaria. "*Liebchen*, I would, if I were going."

Marlborough blinked. "We're staying?"

Dietrich nodded, but kept his gaze on Annamaria. "I'm tired of wandering through the belt, from job to job, scraping by. I'm tired of living in eighty cubic meters. I want to stay in one place for a while. I want to stay one place with you."

Francisca set her fists on her hips. "Why the hell should I let you stay?"

"You need protection. I won't skim too much money. Ninety percent of your platinum proceeds, that's all."

Emergency hatches seemingly slammed shut in Francisca's mind, letting the softer and weaker parts vent to vacuum. She laughed. "What a generous offer."

Dietrich's gaze turned cold, and his fingers tapped his pistol's stock. "It's not negotiable."

Her heart thudded. She couldn't cross the three meters between them before he could fire. What else could she do?

"This is wrong," Annamaria said. "You didn't say anything about this!"

"I wanted to surprise you," Dietrich said. "It's what you want."

"It is not!" Annamaria sounded frantic. "What are you thinking?"

He turned to her. "You're a naïve girl. You'll appreciate—"

Francisca flapped toward Dietrich. If she could grab his pistol—

"—me later. No, Señora."

Francisca suddenly couldn't move. She drifted toward him, but her arms were locked at the back of her stroke. He'd hacked her interface, and overridden her ability to control her body! Panic flooded her, but she still couldn't move. She slowly rotated. Marlborough came into view, with a shocked expression on er face.

Damned machine. Francisca tried to speak. At least Dietrich allowed her to use her voice. "You've got what you wanted," she said to the arēs. "Another chance to victimize us."

"I'm sorry—"

"Don't you dare lie." She drifted on, between Dietrich and the arēs. She jumped to a camera view of the courtyard. She could almost picture this as a nightmare, seeing her body from outside, with an inhuman monster whose presence was unremarkable. If only she could wake up.

— I had no idea he would do this,—e told her. She sensed e spoke privately,that Dietrich was not tapped in.—Believe me, please.—

She returned her attention to her eyes' inputs. E wanted to be forgiven; it showed in er face. What a foolish greedy desire.—What difference would believing you make? It wouldn't change the tradeoff facing you.—

— Tradeoff?—

Behind her, Dietrich and Annamaria argued.—You want to believe you have no guilt,—Francisca told the arēs.—You were just following orders. Yet it chafes against your awareness of your free will. So you want to believe you have the power to choose your actions, but that belief makes you suffer too. It brings back all your guilt.

— Pick one, machine, and spare me your desire to have it both ways.—

Her body's rotation turned her face away from the arēs. E slid to the left of her vision. Er face carried an expression like a human wanting to avoid a difficult decision.

The mind behind the face, though, wasn't human. She could forget that most of the time, but not, suddenly, now. Through the interface and er face's musculature, Marlborough showed, involuntarily, how rapidly e thought. E weighed the question in less than a second, and at the far end of it er certainty leaked through the interface to Francisca. Er decision in that second was as solid and unchanging as the convictions instilled in er since er assembly. Forget e didn't think like humans? She'd never known.

"We're not doing this," Marlborough said. Dietrich must not have heard. He spoke with Annamaria, and the camera showed his profile, his expression somewhere between anger and persuasion. Annamaria ducked her head and hunched her shoulders, but glared with dismay. Marlborough repeated erself, more loudly. Annamaria looked up.

Dietrich turned his head and grinned. "Marley, what the hell?"

"It's wrong. We signed a contract. We have to honor it."

Dietrich lost his grin. "We have to survive."

"We'll survive without this."

Dietrich's vest puffed, and he drifted closer to the robot. "Marley, it's more than survival. Think of offspring. Once we're in control here, we can build them for you."

Marlborough matched er master's gaze for a moment, but then the arēs blinked and bowed er head. The skin around er eyes fell. Through the interface, Francisca felt er be stretched between two poles, between commitment to the right path and a downward spiral into a cluster of neurons that formed a compulsion somewhere between habit and addiction.

Not unlike how she thought of Oskar, crossed her mind, but she had no time now. She had one chance to save her people, and the words came to mind unfiltered by consciousness. "He could, but he wouldn't. Marlborough, you'd be as far from getting reproduced as you are now."

"Shut up," Dietrich said to her.

"Señora, what do you mean?"

"He has no intention of ever reproducing you," Francisca said. "He doesn't need more robots than you."

"Shut the hell up!"

"To be honest, neither do we," Francisca went on. "But there are hundreds of settlements like ours, small and underdefended, who would welcome your descendants. The choice is—" Her voice cut off, and she raggedly exhaled.

Red splotched Dietrich's face. "I told you to shut the fuck up!"

Saliva droplets flew from his mouth. "Now, Marley, let's complete—goddamn you—"

Francisca had rotated around and now saw them both through her eyes. Dietrich and Marlborough stared at each other, like *banditos* in the old movies her father had watched. But this duel was fought between their brains. Francisca felt stray thoughts cross her mind, as the European and the arēs probed each other's interface. Dietrich's arms jerked uselessly, and sweat sheened on his forehead. Heat shimmered around Marlborough's cooling wings.

"Stop. Now," Dietrich said through gritted teeth. "Don't make me—"

Dietrich made a throw in their mental judo bout, she guessed. His right arm smoothly drew his pistol and fired at Marlborough. The courtyard strobed like lightning had struck, and a loud crack echoed. A green spot hung in Francisca's vision, and the air smelled of hot dust and burnt plastic.

The laser had pierced Marlborough's torso and opened a wound in one of er wings. E bled pale blue coolant. The bubbling hot droplets drifted through the room.

Despite er wound, the arēs kept its impassive gaze on Dietrich. E set his arms again to twitching. His heart pounded, and a frantic look came to his face as he gasped for breath the arēs denied him. His heart beat a few more times, arhythmically, from almost stopped to racing, until finally it did stop. His muscles twitched a few more times, and his throat rattled as he died.

Marlborough needed the infirmary. The repair shop? Francisca called through the interface to some trashbirds to help get Marlborough to the latter place, and then turned to the arēs. "How are you?"

Coolant kept bubbling out of er wounds, faster than before. Francisca flapped closer, and winced when the hot droplets brushed her skin. Marlborough's face had a sad look, with er gaze fixed on Dietrich's dead staring eyes. "I won't survive."

"We'll compress the wounds—"

"Coolant lines within my body have been nicked. I would leak internally. There are too many nicked lines, I think, to fix them all."

"We'll get you to the repair shop."

"It won't help, Señora. My mind is dissolving even now. Heat is melting my circuits and impairing their current flows."

E sounded peaceful, but was that only an artifact of er brain damage? "We'll repair you," Francisca said. Where were the trashbirds? She could fly with one hand, if need be, and hook the arēs with the other.

"Even if I could be saved, I don't deserve to survive."

She touched er chin, and turned er head till their gazes met. "He shot you. You were justified—"

"I should have known. He'd attempt this, I should have known. Protect you. I should have—"

"You did what you could," Francisca said. "More than you owed us." Er mind was going, and if she were going to say it it had to be now. "You'll have offspring."

E looked at her, and er face showed fading lucidity. "*Kennen wir uns einander, gnädige Frau?*" Translation software fed an echo of er voice to Francisca's auditory nerve. Do we know each other, my lady?

"You have rendered us a greater service than we had cause to expect. You are a fit template for the next generation. We'll assemble many offspring with brains based on yours. We'll provide them to settlements throughout the belt."

"*Entschuldigen Sie mir, bitte, aber ich spreche kein Spanisch,*" Marlborough said, and then the armatures under er face lost their tone and babbling monosyllables came from er mouth. By the time the trashbirds came in, er speaker had fallen silent and the hum of er powerplant had faded and then stopped. Francisca remained with her palm cradling er cheek, until her daughter's hand rested on her shoulder.

# Pase de un Día

The only displacement booth in San Lorenzo stood between the town hall and the church, where Calle Benito Juárez ended at Calle Progresso. The sky was pale in the east, but the sun had not yet risen over the Sierra Madre, when Chalo ran his hand over sleeping Berto's hair, kissed Adelina, and left their three-room house. Awakening birds chirped behind corrugated iron fences. Chalo's stomach felt hollow. He ignored it. Once he got to work, he would scavenge his morning meal from the previous day's pastries in the break room. His family needed the pesos he would save by doing so.

A few blocks from the displacement booth, he stopped at an intersection, looked left and right, and started across. A car horn blared, startling him, and he jumped back toward the corner. A big, old pickup running on the battery of its hybrid engine had come up behind him and now turned left across his path. The window was down and the driver showed a pudgy face with a scraggly mustache and a medium complexion. "Fucking Indian, you're so short I almost hit you!" The pickup's gasoline engine kicked in and the mestizo roared away, flinging pebbles of crumbling asphalt from his rear tires.

For a moment, a tiny flame of rage burned in Chalo's chest, and he hunched his shoulders and head over it. But rage at the mestizo would not build a better life for his son. He took a deep breath to snuff the smoldering emotion, then looked all ways before crossing the now-empty street.

Soon he passed the private school run by the gray-haired gringo couple. The gate stood ajar. From within came the sound of metal shutters rolling up and English spoken too fast for him to follow. *"Aiden wants us to come for dinner Friday to meet Nadezhda,"* said a woman's voice.

Friday. Did she ask her husband about the deposit deadline at the end of next week? Chalo counted days and hours and his wage, then multiplied them together. He would work every day but Sunday. He would have enough to pay the deposit and get Berto away from the incompetent teacher who slept all day at the government school. The Virgin had blessed Chalo with a son of great intelligence, but her blessing demanded Chalo provide Berto with every possible chance for his intelligence to thrive.

The sun had crested the Sierra Madre, but the church's shadow still covered the displacement booth when he arrived. The booth was a glass cylinder big enough for a family to stand together. Its door showed the laser-etched logo of Teletransportes Mexicanos. A ring of lights around the cylinder's top glowed green. When he opened the door, it swung so easily it seemed to push itself against his hand.

He took his trifold wallet from the inner pocket of his jacket. Old when Adelina had bought it at a flea market, the wallet's folds showed years of wear and the bottoms of the inner slots had long ago split, revealing the edges of his debit card and family photos. Mounted on the inner wall of the booth, opposite the door, were a card reader and a touchscreen. Chalo swiped his debit card and alphanumeric buttons appeared.

With one finger, he tapped out *u-s-d-a-y-p-a-s-s*, then *Introducir*. The next screen asked him to confirm the address and the fee. He touched *Sí*.

He flicked into another booth, twin to the first. He turned and stepped out into a broad, high-ceilinged room, crowded with people and echoing with a babel of voices. This place still made him nervous — he widened his eyes and jerked his head — but he had been through here a few days now and knew the routine. He'd flicked into one of a row of twenty booths standing along what guessed was the south wall. Five queues snaked around plastic railings and aimed for a far wall dominated by an immense United States flag. He went to the nearest queue and shuffled forward.

Most of the people around him were mestizos, with a few blacks and fewer Indians. Regardless of race, many were dressed, like him, in dark trousers and matching tee shirts bearing restaurant logos stitched on the front and displacement booth addresses printed across the back. Chalo heard multiple Spanish dialects; a nasal language that almost sounded like Spanish; and lilting English from some of the blacks. The languages of the other Indians were completely unintelligible. Did everyone from all the countries of the Americas who traveled to the United States on the *pase de un día*, the day pass, come through this border station?

When he was third in line from the checkpoint, Chalo slid his day pass from his wallet. The day pass' white face and red and blue accents were the only things to distinguish it from his debit card. Its English words made little sense to him–he could pick out *United States*, but little else. His printed name seemed to shift in three dimensions when he wiggled the card.

In front of him, a mestiza with a long nose, bunned hair, and a buttoned gray jacket turned her left shoulder toward the turnstile's scanner. *You should consider an implant instead of the card*, the gringo in the consular office had told him in a formal Mexico City accent. *It's more secure.*

Chalo had disregarded his words. If the consular official wanted him to take an implant, it must give the gringos some benefit over him. He understood cards. Even if the card were less secure, he would not lose it.

The turnstile snapped shut behind the mestiza, and the robot torso mounted to the turnstile snaked out its neck and turned its cold, peering face down to Chalo. He shrank from it, more than any morning since his first one through here. His heart thudded and his hand shook as he swiped his day pass through a card reader. *Blessed Virgin, Queen of Mexico, strengthen me....* His hand steadied and he stood a little taller. The robot was only a machine, no different than it had been on earlier days. The near-miss by the pickup in San Lorenzo had made him jumpy.

After a moment, the robot withdrew and a light shone green next to the turnstile. Chalo went through. Around him, a few people strode from the turnstiles toward a row of a dozen displacement booths. The booths looked the same as the one in San Lorenzo, except their doors bore the logos of different companies: Pelton Industries, JumpShift, FARcast, and Portkey Science, alternating in that order. All worked the same, he'd been told, and he'd discovered for himself over his first three days using the day pass. He hadn't yet used a JumpShift booth, so Chalo went to that company's nearest one.

The touchscreen held a swirl of pale blue dots on a darker blue background. It showed three white buttons, each bearing an icon: a red cross for a hospital, a blue shield for police, and a bright yellow dot racing around an outline of the United States. The border police. Going to any of those addresses would waste many of his twelve hours, or worse.

He moved his day pass to one end of the card reader slot. He had been told his debit card, because of its link to an account with a Mexican bank, would not work on the United States network. True or false, he had no need to experiment. He had to get to his job.

Chalo ran his card through the reader. The touchscreen's buttons wobbled and disappeared, and lines of text replaced them.

*Destination/destino: The Shoppes at Indian Bend (NW service booth), Paradise Valley, AZ*

*Latest departure time/Última hora de la salida: 05:49:28 PM MST* and the second ticked up to *29* by the time Chalo pressed the button *Yes/Sí*.

He flicked to work. Concrete block and hanging fluorescent lights defined a wide, empty concourse. Only a robotic mop-and-bucket occupied the space. Its mop slid back and forth over the concrete floor. Chalo turned to the right, heading for a glass door leading to the pedestrian mall. His black sneakers squeaked from the mop's damp residue.

From a large cargo booth behind him came the thudding sounds of its door locking and unlocking. Chalo glanced over his shoulder to see who, or what, had flicked in. From the booth rolled a robotic flatbed cart with a structure at the front for its batteries and its computer brain. Its cargo-handling arms were folded against the structure. On quiet tires, it went the other direction down the concourse, bound for the rear entrance of some boutique, bearing a stack of recycled cardboard boxes marked *Fabrique en France*.

The glass door opened for Chalo. The sky overhead was blue, but the pedestrian mall remained in shadow. Even so, the air was hotter and drier than home and would only grow more so during the day. Chalo began to sweat in his jacket as he followed the winding mall. Most of the shops he passed were closed, their dim interior lights and the dawn glow combining to illuminate window displays of men's suits, ornate jewelry, lingerie, golf clubs. Hidden loudspeakers played orchestral music and water splashed down statues of nudes in the fountains. In front of a perfume store, a sweet floral scent filled his nose.

A glow of lights spilled from a store's front windows onto pavers still in shadow. The sign overhead read *Riviera Maya Coffee & Chocolate Co.* Chalo went in.

A few customers, older men in polo shirts, sat scattered among the tables. They glanced up as Chalo passed, then returned their attention to their tablets. The door from the kitchen swung open, and Hernán approached with a black lacquered tray bearing a cappuccino and a chocolate croissant. He wore a black bowtie, a white jacket, and an imperious look. "You're late," he muttered in Spanish.

Alarmed, Chalo looked at the clock. "It's not yet six."

"That thing does not synchronize properly with the atomic clock. Señor Kaufmann is waiting." Hernán lifted his chin and went to one of the customers.

Through the kitchen, in the break room, Chalo quickly signed in on a touchscreen, moved his wallet to his back pocket, and hung his jacket. He found Kaufmann in his small, windowless office. "I'm sorry I am late, sir."

Kaufmann blinked over his reading glasses, then checked the time display on his tablet. "A few minutes until six. You have the proper attitude. Less than a week and you already understand how the better sort of gringos view time." Kaufmann himself looked like a gringo, pink-white skin and grizzled gray-brown hair, yet he spoke Spanish with an accent native to northern Mexico. It was not Chalo's place to ask if Kaufmann had grown up in Phoenix or Monterrey.

"Better to be five minutes early," Kaufmann went on, "than five minutes late. Remember that."

"I will, sir."

Kaufmann glanced at his tablet. "Three complete days, and you've done adequately so far. Your speed and quality metrics at bussing tables and helping in the kitchen are above average for a trainee."

Chalo had not known. Hernán had continually criticized his work. "Sir, thank you."

Kaufmann's face grew more serious, and he waggled a finger. "But you must not rest. You must approach every job with the idea of always improving. There are ten million Mexican men who would be above average trainees. Do you understand me?"

"I do, sir. I will always improve."

"And hang on to your day pass. I don't know why people squander their opportunity by losing it." He nodded toward the swinging doors to the kitchen. "It's time for you to get to work. Señor Halford has probably left for the golf course by now. His table needs bussing."

Chalo's duties gave the day a steady rhythm, and shifting sunlight and the flow and ebb of customers gave it a melody. He listened to the customers as he carried bins of dirty cups and plates to the robotic dishwasher in the kitchen. Though he understood few words, he wanted to learn all he could about the customers. It would help him improve at his job. And just maybe—a dream so close to impossible he could tell no one, not even Adelina; but thanks to the Virgin, it was possible enough—he might learn how to introduce Berto into their world.

First came doctors and nurses in blue scrubs, stopping at the take-away counter before their morning hospital shifts. Chalo heard the names of gringo cities, names just last week as mythic as El Dorado and Cibola, but now spoken by people a flick away from Seattle, Chicago, Los Angeles. Business people made up most of the crowd between seven and nine, men in three-piece suits, women in skirts and heels. They were often distracted, paying attention to conversations going through their earpieces.

*"We absolutely cannot compromise any aspect of our handicraft certifi-*

*cation,"* one businessman said, chopping the air with his hand to emphasize his words. *"If we falsely pass something as handmade and word gets out, our competitors will eat our lunch. No, I don't care what the elder told you. You tell him we can get the same goddamn rugs from the next village...."*

By late morning, the crowd had thinned. Most customers now were older women wearing tight faces and pantsuits modeled by mannequins in the windows of nearby boutiques. The women came in accompanied by blasts of dry, bakingly hot air.

*"Yes, isn't this place marvelous? Far better than that robotic swill from the Seattle chain. The flour comes from nitrogen-fixing grains, certified fertilizer-free and they preserve so much habitat compared to the genetically unimproved varieties. The coffee and chocolate are fair trade. And all the employees are* Maya from the Yucatan."

Maya from the Yucatan? Had she recently vacationed in Cancún? Chalo shrugged and took another bin of dirty plates to the kitchen. He fed the contents to the dishwasher while Hernán picked up a tray of coffees and pastries laid out by articulated robot arms mounted on tracks in the ceiling.

After a swell of customers stopping by on their way from their lunch hours back to their jobs, the crowd thinned again. Chalo ate a quick lunch of two hard-boiled eggs and a whey protein bagel while standing in a corner of the kitchen. Hernán's scowl lashed him into wolfing down his last bites and hurrying out to the dining room with his bin.

The next customer spike came around three: mothers relaxing for fifteen minutes before picking up children from school, groups of teenagers grousing about homework before pulling out their tablets to study together. Among the latter was a table of two boys. One, pure gringo, sported spiky blond hair and a narrow beard. An animated college logo looped on his tee shirt. His demeanor mixed the privilege of high status, guilt at the privilege, and an earnest desire to reconcile the two. The other was a slender mestizo in his early teens, in a school uniform of khakis and a blue polo. He gulped down one of the coffee cakes the older boy ordered, then looked bored. A tablet set down between them showed the logo of an agency or service called *Tutor For*

*America.*

"*Alfonso, describe the Thirtieth Amendment to the Constitution,*" the gringo boy said.

The younger boy frowned at his chocolate smoothie. "*Let's see. That's the one that gave Washington, D.C. two senators and a congressman?*"

The gringo boy's smile froze. "*That was the Twenty-ninth.*"

"*The Thirtieth. Something about citizenship?*"

"*That's right…. Citizenship and birthright….*"

The younger boy reached for the tablet. "*Can I look it up?*"

"*There are things its good to have in your mind and not just electronically.*"

"*I can't remember. I give up.*"

The older boy sagged with an exhaled breath. "*The Thirtieth Amendment clarified the Citizenship Clause of the Fourteenth. Someone gets citizenship at birth only if both their parents are citizens or legal residents of the United States.*"

"*Why do I need to know this stuff? It's not on the SAT. My dad doesn't use this crap to run his restaurants. He'll give me a good job when I'm done with school. You're wasting my time.*"

The gringo boy blinked in confusion for a moment. "*I know it seems like a waste now… but your father worked to get your name in the lottery for tutoree slots and do you want to tell him you don't care?*"

The younger boy looked away and folded his arms. "*Fine….*"

"*Now, where were—whoa!*"

Chalo turned his head. A large white blur, then the smack of another body colliding with his. The bin slipped from his grip as he fell on his rear end. Cups and plates clattered on the floor, spilling dregs of coffee and crumbs of pastries. A cappuccino flowed around shards of porcelain. It had left tan drops on Hernán's pants when it fell.

The waiter glared down at Chalo. "You stupid fucking Indian!" His voice carried through the now-silent café.

Chalo's cheeks felt hot. "I'm sorry." He scrambled onto his knees and groped for broken cups and plates.

Motion in the corner of his eye resolved into Señor Kaufmann. "What's going on here?"

"This inept Indian didn't watch where he was going," Hernán said.

Chalo's face felt even hotter. What would this do to his numbers? Would Kaufmann fire him on the spot? He flung porcelain fragments into his plastic bin. Sharp slivers scratched his fingertips.

"That is not the full story," the gringo boy said in slow but correct Spanish. "Both men were looking the other way when they ran into each other."

Hernán clamped his lips together. He glowered at the gringo boy for a moment before it seemed he decided better of it. With a milder expression, he said, "I recall looking straight ahead, and even if I didn't, Chalo should watch for me, not I for him."

Kaufmann looked frustrated. "First we fix the problem. Later we find what went wrong and keep it from happening again. You lost an order, Hernán? Replace it and comp the customer. Then help Chalo clean up if he isn't done by then."

Hernán looked sullen, then stalked off to the kitchen. Chalo picked up more shards of cups and plates and mopped up spilled coffee with a tea towel.

*"What did you say?"* the younger boy asked the gringo.

*"That it wasn't the busboy's fault."* His eyes narrowed and his lips parted, as if he wanted to ask a question.

*"What's that look? You think I'm supposed to speak Spanish?"*

In the gringo boy's face, guilt overwhelmed privilege. *"No, no, of course not. Let's get back to work. Where were we, Alfonso?"*

*"You know I want to be called Al...."*

Chalo hurried to the kitchen with a full bin. Hernán passed him and gave a cold stare. Chalo hustled to the trashcan and shook the broken pieces out of the bin. A cold feeling washed through him. He had lost his job. He had failed Berto. He–

He would do his best, even if today was his last day here. Chalo stood a little straighter and returned to the dining room.

Walking near the table with the two boys, someone said, "Señor."

Was Kaufmann still about? Chalo hurried on.

"Señor!" It was the gringo boy, and he called for him. Chalo stopped and faced him, but, uncertain how he could respond, said nothing.

"Your wallet." The gringo boy pointed to the floor near the collision site. It must have fallen from Chalo's pocket when he'd landed on his rear end. Minutes ago and he hadn't noticed!

Chalo hesitated, then set down his bin and picked up the wallet. Still barely intact, but it seemed to be in one piece. Wobbly with relief, he shoved it into his hip pocket and bobbed his head at the gringo boy. "Gracias." He tried his English. "Thank. You."

"You're welcome." The gringo boy looked pleased with himself. Chalo picked up the bin and hurried to the nearest unbussed table. A few words from the younger boy reached him when he was still close enough. *"Five billion third worlders want jobs in America, and the owner can't find one who speaks English?"*

Five o'clock brought the last burst of customers, as the after-work crowd filled the tables around the two boys. Chalo eyed the clock. He would have about twenty minutes from the end of his shift until his day pass would expire. Enough time, but he couldn't dawdle.

At five-thirty, Chalo tossed his last load of dirty plates to the dishwashing robot, then went into the break room. Hernán listened sullenly to Kaufmann. "…That's all, Hernán."

"I'm going to take my break now." Hernán turned and scowled at Chalo, then went into the kitchen and turned for the service doors leading to the rear concourse.

Chalo shuffled closer to the office. "My shift is over, Señor Kaufmann. I must return home while my daypass is good. If you want me to return tomorrow."

Kaufmann frowned. "Why would I not? The spilled plates? Accidents happen and you're within tolerances." He tapped his fingers on his tablet. "Let's keep it that way. Until tomorrow." He chopped the air with his hand as a businesslike wave. Chalo tapped his code on the wall-mounted touchscreen to clock out for the day, then hurried toward the displacement booth.

Heat baked him less than two meters from the front doors. He walked a few minutes toward the late afternoon sun, passing the two boys in the window of a teen clothing store. Chalo squinted, and moved his jacket from arm to shoulder in hopes of finding a spot where it would trap less heat against him. Opening the door to the service concourse gave him a relief. The service concourse lacked air conditioning, but being windowless, was slightly cooler than the outside.

He went in the displacement booth and dug his wallet from his pocket. Open it up and—where was his daypass?

Chalo rifled through his debit card and his family photos, then again. If it wasn't there…. He must have put it in the wrong slot after flicking in that morning. He checked the currency slot and found only his few, worn dollars and pesos. In one of his pants pockets? His jacket pocket? He plunged his hands into all in turn. No daypass.

Panic climbed up the inside of his chest. If he'd lost his daypass, he would have to flick to the U.S. border guards. They would send him home, but he would lose any chance for another daypass. A billion men could be above-average trainees, but his son would languish another year in the government school, and that year might be enough to smother Berto's intelligence forever–

Breath deeply. Retrace your steps. Your wallet never left your pocket, except when you collided with Hernán.

He checked the time on his phone. About fifteen minutes until his daypass expired. He ran out of the concourse. His feet pounded down the sun-baked mall. Chalo veered to avoid a pair of tall gringas peering down their narrow noses at him, which brought into his view the gringo boy and the one being tutored.

A sudden idea made him stumble to a stop. A mix of English and Spanish spilled from his mouth. "Señor, favor, please, mi wallet, mi daypass, pase de un día, is fall out–"

The gringo boy took a moment to recognize him. "Oh, you're the busboy," he replied in Spanish. "You lost your daypass? It was in your wallet when you collided with the waiter? It looks like a credit card, yes?" His wince showed sympathy. "I'm afraid I didn't see it anywhere on the floor in the café."

Chalo's face slumped. Frustration tightened his mouth and lowered his brows. He glanced at the mestizo boy. Had this one seen something? He would have to tell. By the Virgin, Chalo would make it clear he had to tell. Chalo stood as tall as he could and drew up to eye level on the boy. Unease panged him as he looked the boy straight in the face. "Did you see it?" Chalo asked in Spanish.

"*What?*" came the reply, in English. The boy grew surly. "No hablo español."

"*Did you see his daypass fall out of his wallet?*" the gringo boy said.

"*Why would I care enough to look? No, I didn't see it.*"

The gringo boy winced in more sympathy. "Neither of us saw it." He looked thoughtful for a moment. "But the waiter passed by the spot soon after everything happened. He might have noticed something."

"Thank you," Chalo said in Spanish. Time was too tight to bother with English. He ran down the mall. Sweat stuck his shirt to his back. The air conditioning inside the café made him shiver.

He went to the tables near where he'd fallen. Customers frowned and he barely noticed as he peered around chair and table legs for a glimpse of white with red and blue accents. Nothing. Frantic, he called to another busboy, "Have you seen Hernán?"

"No." The other busboy kept filling his bin.

"He's on break," said Kaufmann. Chalo's eyes widened in alarm. Kaufmann would not want to be bothered with his problem. "Why do you need him? You should be on your way home."

Again, the Virgin helped Chalo stand straight. "I lost my daypass. Sir, it was in my wallet, I swear to you it was, I wouldn't lose it for a stupid reason, but it must have fallen out when I fell down after running into Hernán and I want to ask if he saw it."

Kaufmann frowned, but Chalo soon realized, not at him. "He should be back from break by now. Come with me." Kaufmann went to the kitchen without a glance behind him. Chalo hurried after. The service doors slid apart and Kaufmann led the way onto the concourse.

"That fucking thing's got five minutes till expiration," said a high male voice in Spanish. "I'd be super lucky to find a hoodlum who needs it to make a getaway. Twenty dollars."

"Alright, I'll take–" Hernán broke off. The other, a slender barrio boy, froze wide-eyed. The barrio boy recovered first; he snatched Chalo's daypass from Hernán's hand and ran down the concourse toward the service booths. His boots thudded on the concrete and his pants slipped down his backside.

"Thieving son of a whore!" Kaufmann shouted as he ran after him. Chalo ran too, but with his shorter legs, fell further behind with each step. The barrio boy looked over his shoulder. The white of his eye stood stark against his skin and black hair. As he looked back at them, he lost his footing and stumbled. Kaufmann tackled him. The barrio boy thudded to the floor, breath whoofing out and the daypass skittering from his hand.

"Take your daypass and go, Chalo," Kaufmann said. "I'll deal with the police."

"Yes, sir." Chalo reached for the card, then gave a look back at Kaufmann and the barrio boy. In the distance, near the service entrance to the café, Hernán was out of sight.

"Go! I need you back here in the morning. It will be a busier day than usual, with one less waiter on staff."

Chalo nodded and ran down the concourse to the displacement booth, muttering an Ave Maria as the daypass dug into his palm.

# Mike Fink Goes to Big Bend

You know, niña, Big Bend used to be very different. No lakes, no forests, no pygmy triceratops and stegosaurs roaming the countryside. No, honest, niña, I wouldn't lie to you. Back at the turn of the century, Big Bend was the dustiest corner of Texas. How did it change? Well...

Mike Fink had worked for a couple hundred years — poling flatboats down the Ohio, running locomotives for the Missouri Pacific, driving a tractor trailer between Juarez and Windsor — so he retired rich. Compound interest, you know. He bought fifty thousand acres in Presidio County, the biggest part of the Big Bend. Nothing grew on his land but dry grass along the highway between Marfa and the Chinati ridge.

Mike, though, had a plan. He took off his shirt, knelt down, and punched the ground. A crater formed under his fist. He turned around and tossed rock fragments into the Pacific. Waves swept over atolls, but Mike paid no mind. He turned back to the fist-sized hole, punched, tossed the fragments out to sea. Forty days he kept at, and extended the hole five hundred miles southeast. Sweat poured off him, and when it dried the wind pushed salt drifts across the highway. Scientists blamed rising sea levels on global warming, instead of the rocks he'd thrown.

Finally, Mike's tunnel reached the Gulf of Mexico near Brownsville. He groped up through sea bottom mud and reached the cold salt water. Yet Mike had a plan for that too. He squeezed his fist around some ocean water, squeezed so hard the water flowed up the tunnel but left the salt behind. He squeezed, again and again, till the veins stood up on his arms and his forehead; but he had fresh water for his fifty thousand acres. He used rubble from the tunnel to dam the water, and planted crops on his land: insect-resistant corn, herbicide-resistant soybeans, blue-gene cotton. Tired from his work, Mike sat on the Chinati ridge, looked north at his land, and rubbed his sore right arm.

Behind him and to the right, gravel popped under tires. Mike turned. Across the river, a black Chevy Suburban with tinted windows and state of Chihuahua license plates pulled up. The driver's door opened, and Principe Oso stepped out on his hind legs. His claws scratched at the ground, and his gold-brown fur shone in the sun. Sunglasses and a vacquero hat don't look good on every bear, but they looked good on him.

"What do you want?" Mike growled.

Principe Oso folded his front legs across his chest. "You've already in trouble, Miguelito. Don't piss me off."

"I ain't done nothing to you."

Principe Oso shook his head, and tapped his paw on the ground. "Your tunnel goes through Mexican soil."

Damn if he wasn't right, but Mike acted nonchalant. "What you going to do about it?"

"I'll dig down to it and cave it in."

Mike swore. Forty days' work down the drain. He rubbed his aching arm again. "Can I make it up to you?"

Principe Oso scratched under his snout with his paw. "You can give me some fresh water."

Mike thought. Sure easier than punching another tunnel all the way to Brownsville. "Deal."

Mike carried water across the river, and Principe Oso planted corn and beans, jalapeños and habañeros, and agave cactus. They became good neighbors. Principe Oso made tequila from his agave, and sold it cheap to Mike. Mike had bear-sized jeans made from his cotton, and gave them to Principe Oso. After six months, they drove to Houston in Principe Oso's Suburban to buy ostrich-leather cowboy boots and visit Rick's Cabaret and the Men's Club.

When they got back, though, the water was gone. "Someone drank up the ponds," Mike said.

"It's the sun, Miguelito."

Of course. The sun shone so hot the ponds had evaporated. "I'll get some more." Mike knelt down and ran his arm down the tunnel. He squeezed out some more fresh water. His arm ached before he was half-done. When he finished, it hurt just to dip chewing tobacco. Maybe he should go to Alaska and get some ice for his shoulder.

"Mike Fink," said a baritone voice.

Mike looked up. John Henry stood near Fort Davis. He wore a short sleeved white dress shirt and a clip-on tie. He scratched the back of his hand on McDonald Observatory, but his brown-eyed stare fixed on Mike.

"John Henry? I thought that steam drill beat you."

"No, Mike, I won the race. Fourteen feet to nine."

"I remember now. And it didn't kill you, either."

John shook his head. "It came damn close. I lay in bed the next morning, more sore than I'd ever been in my life, and I realized something. Machines were getting stronger all the time. Men weren't."

A twinge in Mike's shoulder made him wince. "You got that right."

"I went to Tuskegee, learned engineering—"

The twinge got worse. Mike gritted his teeth and rubbed his shoulder. John smiled, and Mike narrowed his eyes. "You want to laugh at me?"

"No, Mike. I want to help you. I know how you're getting your fresh water, and all I can think is, that's what steam drills are for. I can build a machine to get the water for you."

Mike rubbed his shoulder. He'd be glad to stop doing such hard work, but all the cash from his latest crops had ended up dancers' G-strings. "Sounds good, but I don't have any money to pay you."

"Forget the money. I'll take fifteen thousand acres."

Mike frowned. "Why do you want to live out here?"

John nodded at the town of Ft. Davis near his feet, at a cluster of adobe huts from the old fort. "My little brother was a buffalo soldier. He died out here fighting the Apaches."

A pretty good reason, Mike had to admit. "If your machine works, you've got a deal."

John Henry built a reverse osmosis desalinization plant where Mike's tunnel met the Gulf. Out came the sweetest water Mike ever tasted. After that, Mike, John Henry, and Principe Oso became good neighbors. After Mike harvested his corn, he fed the silage to John's cattle. John gave the others fresh steaks every week. A year later, Mike and John drove to Chihuahua city for Principe Oso's wedding to La Llorona. Mike had heard bad things about her first marriage, but it had been five hundred years since she'd drowned that two-timing conquistador's children: cognitive therapy and Prozac had helped her a lot. They partied all night in the ballroom of the Chihuahua Omni.

When Mike and John, hungover on tequila, got back to Big Bend, they found the corn withered and the ponds dry. "The pump went bad?" Mike asked.

John checked the data feed from the desalinization plant. "It burnt out from pumping too fast."

"The sun wasn't strong enough to evaporate water that quick." Mike's eyebrows rose, but his head still pounded. "Someone drank it. And I know how to find out who."

After Principe Oso and La Llorona got back from their honeymoon in Cozumel, Mike drained his ponds and filled them with Principe Oso's tequila. Then they all drove to Houston for a weekend shopping at the Galleria.

When they came back, they found Coyote passed out on the bank of an empty pond. Mike held him down and splashed water on his face till he woke up.

"What do you think you're doing?" Mike said. "It's private property. You can't drink my water."

Coyote squinted at him. "What am I supposed to do? I don't have any water of my own. The men from Washington stuck me on the driest land around."

"That doesn't mean you can steal mine," Mike said. Maybe there was another answer. "Can't you sell something for money to buy water?"

"Sell? Well, there used to be uranium deposits on the reservation—"

"There you go," La Llorona said.

"—but when the men from Washington found out about them, they redrew the boundaries of the rez."

John Henry sniffed out a breath. "You call yourself a trickster?"

Coyote shook his head. "I didn't go to law school. Back to my point. I have nothing to sell. All I have is the hundred sunniest square miles of southern New Mexico."

Mike's gaze met those of John Henry, Principe Oso, and La Llorona. All their faces lit up with realization.

"Install photovoltaic cells, and sell 30 gigawatt-hours a year of solar electricity," John said.

"Build a year-round golf resort, modeled after the best 18 holes in the world." Principe Oso mimed a swing.

"Get a Chinese company to make tribal handicrafts you can sell on the internet," La Llorona added.

Mike shrugged. "Hell, just open a casino."

Coyote frowned. "Those are all good ideas, but it takes money to make money."

Mike looked around, and the others nodded before he had to ask them. "We can loan you what you need to get started."

Coyote thought for a moment, then held out his front paw to them. "Deal."

# THE THIRTIETH AMENDMENT

*1. The first sentence of the first Section of the Fourteenth Amendment is hereby repealed and replaced with the following:*

*Any person born in the United States to parents who are both citizens or permanent legal residents of the United States and are subject to the jurisdiction thereof, or any person naturalized in the United States, is a citizen of the United States and of the State wherein he or she resides.*

*2. Any person under the age of eighteen years who is now living, who was born to at least one parent who was neither a citizen nor a permanent legal resident of the United States, and who was considered a citizen of the United States under the first sentence of the first Section of the Fourteenth Amendment as of the date of ratification of this Amendment, shall have the right to live and work in the United States, upon attaining the age of eighteen years and demonstrating fluency in the English language.*

Gonzalo's stomach flopped like a beached fish gasping for breath. The waiting room was a plain place of vinyl tile, paneling the color of caramel, and hard, misshapen plastic chairs. The only sounds came from the shifting bodies of the other twenty-two test takers and the rustle of traffic on the twelve-lane freeway a kilometer away. The United States flag hung on a pole at the front of the room, next to a picture of President Benchley, as stern as an angry saint.

Gonzalo glanced around the room. Here he was in Los Angeles, just two hundred kilometers from Mexico, but only three other test-takers looked Latin American, let alone Mexican. Four looked like Arabs—in the corner, two *negros* with brown-black skin—there were even two *rubios*, brother and sister, perhaps, blond hair and blue eyes set in wide faces. But the greatest number were *chinos*. What word did the *americanos* use? Orientals? Asians?

One *chino*, black hair spiked over a face dominated by thick-rimmed eyeglasses, spoke to the *rubio* brother. "My father, big man in party, send my mother to luxury birth hospital, Orange County."

"*Da,*" said the *rubio*, then muttered something in a foreign language.

"My father bring in test prep tutor. From U.S. Spend top dollar." The *chino* smelled of cologne and cigarettes. "I ready."

Gonzalo's stomach turned more sour. Test prep tutor? He couldn't compete with that. All he'd done to learn English was press the CC button on television shows from San Diego. And check out books from the *americano* missionary library on Avenida Benito Juarez, books with pictures about FIFA World Cups and auto repair.

He took a breath. He didn't compete against the *chino*. It only mattered how many questions he answered right.

He glanced around again. His gaze met that of the one Latina in the room. Clear skin and black hair shiny under the fluorescent lights in the ceiling. Beautiful, but who was he to say she was too beautiful for him? He gave her a confident look. Her gaze lingered on his for a long moment, then coyly turned away.

After he started his own auto repair shop, he'd scrub the grease from under his fingernails and find her.

A door opened next to the picture of President Benchley. Every-one in the waiting room looked up. In came a tall *gringo* with stooped shoulders and a stubbly brown beard. "It's almost time to enter the testing room. Follow me."

Gonzalo and the others formed a single file and passed the *gringo* into the next room. Three rows of lockers covered the far wall. Keys with orange handles and elastic coils hung from each lock. A short *negra*—no, the *americano* missionaries, *gringo* boys in white shirts and black neckties, had told him never to call them by the Spanish words, he should instead always say *African-American* — stood with fists on her wide hips and gave orders. "Phones, smart watches, papers, books, pens, pencils, backpacks, purses, wallets, anything else you got, you put it in a locker. You get it back after the test. I'm going to say it again, phones, smart watches, anything you can use to send a message in or out, anything you might have something written down on, you cannot bring it in the test room. The only exception is that sealed packet you got from the U.S. embassy or consulate in your home country. Everything else goes in a locker."

The file broke up into a mass of people scrambling for the lockers. Gonzalo followed the Latina, but the *chino* stinking of cigarettes got in his way. Gonzalo found a locker at the end, turned the key, opened the door. He placed his wallet and his touchscreen phone inside. They looked tiny in the moment before he shut the door.

"Next," said the African-American woman, with a flick of her head to toss her long straight hair, "you're going to hand over your sealed packet and we're going to prick your finger for DNA. It ain't going to hurt. We got to do this to match you with who the packet says you are. Alright, line on up."

From the back of the line, Gonzalo craned his head. The African-American woman sat at a table near another door. With her at the table was a *china* in blue scrubs and black hair tied up in a bun. She wore rubber gloves and racks of medical supplies rested on the table in front of her.

The line crept forward, but fairly quickly. When Gonzalo's turn came, he handed the packet to the African-American woman. The *china* in blue scrubs swabbed his left index finger's tip with a cooling wipe, then squeezed his finger with one hand. He barely felt the pin prick. The *china* touched one end of a slender, two-centimeter long glass straw to the drop of blood. When blood filled the glass straw, she dropped it into a plastic tube, snapped the tube's lid closed, and sealed the lid with a sticker bearing a bar code and his name. A matching sticker resealed his packet.

They worked hard to prevent anyone from cheating.

"Go on in," the African-American woman said. She gestured at the door to the next room. Two men stood to the sides of the door. *Gringos* with buzzcut hair and bulky black vests with the ICE logo on the breast.

Gonzalo bristled—his first memory was of men like them, ordering his mother and him onto a bus bound for Tijuana—but they didn't even notice. Who were they to—

He took another breath. Nothing he could do about that now. Except pass the test.

The testing room held four rows of six chairs with flipped-open desks. Plastic-wrapped wires tied each chair to the floor, and cords tied to each chair a tablet computer in a rubberized case resting on each desk. Only two desks were empty. The distant freeway sounded much quieter. The stooped, bearded *gringo* stood near the door with a different tablet in his hand. "Name?" he asked.

Gonzalo gave his. Why did he have to? He must be the last one on the list.

The *gringo* checked the tablet. "You're on the list. Sit there." He pointed at a chair in the third row, second from the right. Next to the *chino* with spiked hair and thick-rimmed glasses.

"I have to?"

"Seats are randomly assigned with a constraint to minimize proximity of people speaking the same native language."

Gonzalo understood a few of the *gringo*'s words. "Assigned. Okay." He went to his seat. The Latina sat on the front row, on the far side of the room, her head bowed over folded hands.

Gonzalo sat. The *chino* lounged back, tablet with dark screen in his right hand. The *chino* shook his wristwatch past the end of his left sleeve. A thick mass of dials wheeled around, and a small diamond glittered in place of the number 12.

*He's not your problem. The test is.*

The door closed. The bearded *gringo* stayed there and the short, wide African-American woman went to the front of the room. She gave instructions about the multiple-choice test, the tablets, they had one hour, no leaving the room. Gonzalo listened carefully.

*Madre de Dios,* he prayed, *help me pass the test.*

"Alright everybody," said the African-American woman. "Begin."

Gonzalo's tablet screen lit up. He pressed *Start*.

The hole in his stomach enlarged. He read and reread the first question.

*Incarceration is to penitentiary as:*

*a. Intoxication is to intermediary.*

*b. Admission is to hospital.*

*c. Departure is to garage.*

*d. Graduation is to university.*

How the hell was he supposed to know all these complicated words? Why couldn't they do this test by speaking? The hole in his stomach sent hot tendrils up his chest. His chance to work in the U.S. was about to collapse.

Gonzalo pressed *a* and shook his head. A glance to the right showed the *chino* staring intently at the screen. His left elbow rested on the desk and he pressed the fingers of his left hand against his forehead. The *chino* entered an answer and kept going.

Gonzalo turned his attention back to his tablet. Question two. Reading comprehension. A passage from one of the *americano* documents, the Constitution or the Declaration. The hot tendrils faded, replaced by something worse, a chill fluid sensation trickling down his throat. He turned dull eyes to the first question.

*According to the signers, what sort of rights are Life, Liberty, and the pursuit of Happiness?*

*a. Rights that only citizens, and not foreigners, have.*

*b. Rights that only human beings, and not alien life forms, have.*

*c. Rights that people can give up in exchange for other rights.*

*d. Rights that cannot be taken from people.*

Gonzalo skimmed the passage again. *Unalienable* might mean not for aliens. But why would the *americano* founders talk about aliens?

Wait, they called *illegales* 'aliens' too. He answered *a* and pressed *next page.*

Three faint buzzes sounded somewhere to his right.

He glanced at the *chino*. A later page of reading comprehension questions. Damn, the *chino* was quick. The private tutor must have been good.

On the first question, the *chino* answered *c*.

Two faint buzzes. Did an insect fly around the room?

The *chino* answered the next question *b*. Then he cast a scowl at Gonzalo.

Gonzalo looked away just as four faint buzzes sounded. They confirmed his guess. They came from the *chino*'s wristwatch. And it looked like the *chino* answered the next question *d*.

The *chino* scowled in Gonzalo's direction. He took his left hand away from his forehead and moved it under the desk. He clamped his lower thighs together on the wristwatch.

How did the *chino* cheat? Maybe his glasses held a tiny camera and a transmitter. His 'private tutor' must wait nearby, read the question, and give him the answers by sending buzzes to the wristwatch.

Gonzalo sighed. Some people had the money and the connections to bend the rules. He didn't. So he wouldn't pass the test. Might as well put the tablet down and take a nap before his bus ride back to Tijuana.

Something solidified in his spine. Hell no. That's how Mexicans thought. They handed the steering wheels of their lives to fate and ended up going nowhere. But a piece of paper from the Los Angeles County Vital Records Office and more paper stamped by a consular clerk in Tijuana said he was an *American*. *Madre de Dios*, he would act like one. Maybe he would lose, like the GIs in some late night movie who were bloodied by Rommel at Kasserine, but he would fight.

He tapped *next page*.

As if in response to his new resolve, the questions got easier. One reading question rephrased a road sign as *a driver will pay twice as much for a speeding ticket*. When applying for a loan to buy a house, he reasonably guessed that the *M* in the acronym *ARM* stood for *mortgage*. He used the knowledge stolen from the *chino* to answer all the multi-question reading comprehension passages with, in order, *c*, *b*, and *d*.

Even after the *chino* finished early and leaned back in his chair, arms folded over his chest, right arm over left to obscure his wristwatch, Gonzalo kept battling. A miser was someone who was unhappy, right? And an author was someone who had authority? Even though doubts came in, he remembered another late-night movie, where young *gringos* and *negros* bonded on a practice field for American football. A coach yelled "play to the whistle."

Gonzalo mashed the *next page* button. Another page of reading comprehension questions, but only two of them. He couldn't use the answers taken from the *chino*. He'd have to read the whole thing.

*The North Atlantic Treaty Organization (NATO)—*

The screen instantly went dark.

"Alright everybody. If you haven't figured it out by now, the testing session is over." The African-American woman raised her eyebrow. If you hadn't figured it out by now, she must think you were very stupid. "The tablet will soon give you your results. If it says you failed, you will leave the room and have 72 hours to return to your countries of residence. If you fail, it isn't the end of the world, you can apply again in three years."

Someone on the front row mumbled a question. The African-American lady answered, loudly, "If you pass, you wait right here while we discharge the others."

Color flashed on all the desks. Gonzalo looked down like everyone else.

His tablet showed a red screen. Under the ICE logo appeared the stark white word *Failed*.

Gonzalo's shoulders fell. Three years before he could try again. Three years behind concrete walls topped with embedded broken bottles, on streets rendered dangerous by dueling *narcos*, working in the auto repair shop for low wages under the harsh shouts of the *jefé*.

The stink of cologne and cigarettes mauled his nose. "You fail," said the *chino*. The tablet on his desk glowed green, read *Passed*. "Too bad. You no be my lawn guy. Ha ha."

Gonzalo's cheeks burned. He turned away from the *chino*. The pressure of seventeen others leaving the room pulled him up and out of the desk. He joined the line of those who'd failed, and trudged toward the exit. Six places ahead of him, the Latina shuffled along, black hair still glossy as it slumped down the sides of her downturned face.

He came to the table just outside the door. Lockers slammed on the other side of the room. The bearded *gringo* asked for his name and found his sealed packet in a basket. The *gringo* opened the packet. A moment later he handed over Gonzalo's birth certificate. "Yours to keep," he said.

Gonzalo took it. Thick paper and English words that seemed empty of meaning. The *americanos* took such stock in such things. Rule of law. Fair play. Naive fools.

Naive fools who won world wars and invented the automobiles he worked on every day.

And thanks to the piece of paper in his hand, he was one of them.

"The *chino* next to me cheated."

The *gringo* looked up. His Adam's apple bobbed in his forward-leaning neck. "Say again?"

"The *chino*—in English should I say Oriental or Chinaman?"

"'Asian.'" The *gringo* reached for a tablet. "What makes you think he cheated?" he asked, while he looked down at a seating chart.

"I heard his wristwatch buzz. Once it buzzed four times, bzz bzz bzz bzz, and he answered *d*. Another time, it buzzed twice, bzz bzz, and he answered *b*. A third time—" Gonzalo broke off. The bearded man's eyes looked like he'd heard enough.

But he had to believe him! "And when he noticed I could tell he was up to something, he put his left hand between his legs, where he could feel the buzz and I couldn't hear it."

The *gringo* raised his left hand. "I'm sure you saw and heard that. And his glasses had thick rims. It might be possible to hide a camera and a transmitter in them."

"So you'll fail him? Make him come back in three years?"

"If he cheated, he's barred from trying again for life. Thank you for bringing the possibility of cheating to our attention. It's very civic-minded of you. Good luck to you when you try again—"

"Possibility?" Gonzalo said. "Aren't you going to investigate?"

"I assure you, we will. If we need to."

Gonzalo rocked back on his heels. *This* was the *americano* rule of law? To favor a, an Asian who cheated over a Mexican who told the truth? "Need to?" he shouted.

A smile distorted the *gringo's* beard. "The second part of the exam is a test of verbal fluency."

"What does that mean?"

The *gringo* raised his palm. "We just tested how well you read and write English. The next test is how well you *speak* it."

Gonzalo's breath caught. He bowed his head, apologizing in his own mind for shouting. "I understand, sir."

"Again, good luck next time."

"Thank you," Gonzalo said, already turning away. The Latina with the long glossy hair stood at an open locker. Her trembling hand gripped the edge of the locker door. She squeezed shut her eyes, trying to close the valve of tears.

Gonzalo lifted his shoulders and went toward her. In three years, perhaps they would try again together.

# AFF*E*CTIVE DISORDER

The biotech company occupied a glass-and-steel lowrise in the manicured pine forests of Houston's northern suburbs.

Albert Jimenez climbed out of his car at the front doors. While it parked itself, he entered a reception area. Terrazzo clacked underfoot, and chrome letters float-mounted and backlit on a curving wall spelled out Aff*E*ctive Technologies.

Why the italics? he mused, while he waited for Rachel Nguyen, the company's general counsel.

Pantsuit, black hair to the shoulder, and an expression on the severe side of the knife-edge professional women had to walk between femininity and authority. Albert shook her offered hand. Smooth skin, warm, not moist. "I'm glad to match a face to your reputation," she said. "Let's go to my office."

In Nguyen's office, file folders lay on her desk like sedimentary strata, and on the credenza, a slideshow of family photos filled the unused monitors. The windows showed pines and the harsh light of a Texas summer day. "Have a seat," Nguyen said, and waved at a chair facing the desk. The leather squeaked as Albert shifted his weight. Nguyen sat in a webbed ergonomic chair on her side of the desk and regarded him.

Half Albert's business came from litigation-support investigations, a euphemism for parties in lawsuits seeking dirt on their opponents.

"What's the case?"

"A few months ago, did you hear about the suicide of Patricia Jameson?"

"I follow the news." An heiress with psych problems. Houston had a thousand of them.

"One thing that hasn't been reported is that she was a test subject in a Phase III trial of our device, AffEctor."

"Device?" Albert asked. "It's not a drug?"

"Not as such. Our device is a tiny biochemical factory — about a cubic millimeter in size — implanted in the brain. It contains an engineered strain of the bacterium *E. coli*. The bacterium name is where the marketing team came up with the typographical trick in the company's." She wrinkled her nose to express her opinion.

Albert frowned. "Wait, *E. coli*? People get sick from exposure to it."

She raised her palm. "Our scientists could explain it more fully. I'll summarize. We've knocked out enough genes to make it harmless. Our *E. coli* can't live outside the device, so there's no risk of a gastroenteritis outbreak from them."

She flicked the air with two fingers. "Enough of what they cannot do. Here's what they can. We engineered them to produce serotonin and endorphins. Those are mood-elevating compounds naturally found in our brains. Over twelve hundred people have used it up to an including our Phase III. Jameson's was our first suicide."

"Her family filed the suit?"

"Her husband. Phillip Jameson. He's alleging wrongful death due to negligence. He wants millions, and so do our outside counsel to defend against him. Which is where you come in."

Albert nodded. Hiring him to unearth Phillip Jameson's secrets would cost AffEctive a tiny fraction of the prospective legal fees and damages.

Nguyen went on. "The worst of it is he helped us get started. His firm, Mizukami and Choudhary, works with biotech start-ups. He asked to get his wife into the trial."

"That sounds irregular."

"It's uncommon," Nguyen said. A pained look formed on her face.

"Your fee is three thousand a day?"

He looked apologetic. "Thirty-five-hundred. The euro's been strong lately. Plus expenses."

Nguyen quirked her mouth, then sighed. "From what I hear, you're worth it. Beam me your contract."

A few moments later she swiped a stylus across her phone, then beamed back an electronically signed copy. Albert glanced at the swirls of her name on his phone's screen, then asked, "Do you have a file started on Phillip Jameson?"

Nguyen nodded. "Yeah, it's…." She turned to her computer, nudged the mouse. A legion of icons held formation on the screen. A few clicks. "Here you go."

"Thanks." His phone bonged with receipt. He swiped through the first few pages. A few general notes on Jameson. Not much to start with.

*Every thing they left out means more work for you*, part of him thought as he went to his car. From the moment it opened its doors for him, shame at the thought dogged him the entire drive home.

The next day found him at a neighborhood pool across town from his house. The diving board thudded, and a young boy shrieked and splashed in, knees drawn to his chest. "Thanks for meeting with me, Maria," Albert said.

"It's no bother — I haven't seen you in ages," she said. Solitary grays streaked her dark brown hair and she rubbed sunscreen into thickened thighs. Men had it lucky, he mused. *At first glance, only our spirits embrittle and sag with age.*

"How's private investigation?" she asked.

He shrugged. "Better than HPD."

She arched her eyebrow. "What does freelancing give you that we didn't?" A faint emphasis rode her tone. He read it to mean she was between relationships again. Her brown eyes looked plaintive, and her gaze wandered over his face, then away.

He ignored her subtext. "Less paperwork. Now what—"

Shouts came from a corner of the pool. Maria leaned forward in her deck chair. A knot of eight-year-olds, her son among them, splashed and grappled. It took her a moment to loosen her grip on the arms of the deck chair. "I'm sorry, you were saying?"

"What can you tell me about Patricia Jameson's suicide?"

She crossed her arms over the stretched spandex waist of her bathing suit. "A lot. But what's in it for me?"

"Credit at the favor bank."

"That's all?" She put on a pout.

"There might come a time when you could use some off-the-books help with an investigation."

She thought about that as a cloud scudded in front of the sun.

"You saw plenty like them," Maria said. "Her husband called 911 about nine-thirty that night to report his wife was dead, apparently suicide. My homicide partner and I got to the house after a patrol car and an ambulance."

"Was he at home when she killed herself?"

"He said he had just returned from work and found her body. A law firm downtown, Matsu-something—"

"Mizukami and Choudhary?"

"That's it. We checked his whereabouts. His ID card showed he'd been in his office building all day, and according to the traffic control transponder in his car, it dropped him off that morning and parked in a garage outsdie downtown all day until he returned home."

"So he's clear."

Maria nodded. "The scene itself was so damn pathetic. One of those big houses on upper Kirby, you know, fifty feet off the street and they don't light up the front yard at night."

"Poor little rich girl," Albert said.

"Yeah, like she could have problems. A husband, no kids, tens of millions in the bank." She shut her eyes. "At the scene, the victim was slumped over on the couch. Silk kimono and underwear, her sphincters relaxed. Woke up and killed herself, it looked like. The coroner put time of death at about two PM."

"Overdose?" The most common means of suicide for an upper-class woman.

Maria nodded. "We found an empty bottle of sleeping pills on the table, and a spilled bottle of cognac on the floor." She shook her head. "How can someone who spends twelve hundred bucks on a bottle of liquor need to kill themselves?"

"How was her husband?" he asked.

"Oh, he was a son of a bitch. He plastered this shocked look on his face, but it was fake. He was glad to be rid of her. And he asked all these questions, was it murder, was it assisted suicide?"

"That's odd." Patricia Jameson had a history of mental illness; surely her husband would have assumed the simplest explanation.

"Yeah, it was so plainly suicide. No note, but there usually isn't. No phone calls in or out; no sign of forced entry or struggle; no one seen by the neighbors or the home security system."

Two girls in baggy waterproof *chadors* — Iranian? Pakistani? — climbed out of the pool and padded to the drink machine. The July sun lifted their footprints off the concrete deck.

"What about her medical implant?" Albert asked.

"Medical implant? Oh, yeah, I remember now. Jameson started talking to himself, stuff like, 'I got her in that trial because I trusted AffEctive. It was supposed to work. Did it fail?' I thought he was talking about a drug until I got the coroner's report. Damn, that's frightening, putting bacteria in your brains to shit out some drug."

"Did Jameson talk about lawsuits?"

"After a few minutes, yeah, he started ranting. 'Were they lying about the safety and efficacy? What were they thinking, screwing with me? I'm a lawyer.' "

Albert scrawled notes on his phone. If Jameson had a lawsuit in mind before his wife's body reached the morgue, AffEctive's defense could argue it as a sign of no emotional distress, meriting reduced damages. But Jameson would trot out enough expert witness psychologists to cloud the jury's mind. Not Albert's problem. He gathered the information; how the attorneys used it justified them earning in an hour what he made in a day.

He sounded her out for more information, but got nothing useful. "Thanks for your time, Maria." He stood.

Her gaze held him. "I'm not looking for something that we both know isn't there, but would you want to get together over drinks sometime? Some things you can only talk about with another cop."

"I'm an ex-cop."

"Getting rid of the badge didn't change you," she said. She un-furled her fingers toward him. "Just a drink."

Her agenda seemed clear—just a drink, leading to sex, followed by enough other booty calls to keep him coming back indefinitely. *Christ, you've gotten more cynical than I recall*, part of him thought.

"I know what you mean about the badge," he said. "Yeah, a beer, sounds good. I'll give you a call when this case cools down."

"Sure." Her smile didn't reach her eyes.


Albert spent the evening in the pale glow of the monitors, hunting the public and semi-private webs for data on the Jamesons. Small won-der Jameson felt relieved the night of his wife's death. Patricia Jame-son had been the only child of John Allocatelli, a storage-peripherals tycoon around the turn of the century. (Two hundred megabytes in twenty cubic centimeters had once been impressively dense. Albert shook his head). Allocatelli had the savvy to sell out to a competitor before Moore's law smashed his business model.

Business savvy, and ill luck. The Allocatellis died in a Zapatista guerrilla attack on their resort on Cozumel, and left Patricia an or-phaned nineteen-year-old multimillionaire. Somehow she'd kept her assets intact against all the distant relatives and financial advisors who must have come out of the woodwork to "help" her manage her inher-itance. Kept intact so that now, between forty and fifty million dollars' worth of stock in computer hardware companies, passed to Jameson. Even today, that was a lot of money. How much more could he need? Oh, no, the lawsuit was about *principle*, bankrupt AffEctive so they can't do this to anyone else. Lawyers with principles. Albert sniffed out a breath.

Patricia Jameson had received treatment for unipolar affective dis-order—call it depression, for Christ's sake—for the two decades since her parents' death. Dozens of medications, multiple psychotherapists, hospitals, experimental treatments…. She had been a money machine for the Houston psychiatric community. Small wonder she was never cured.

His web searches dug up more dirt on Jameson. A couple of speeding tickets, an IRS audit. Not enough. He went through an anonymizer to try remotely logging into the database of Mizukami and Choudhary, but security stonewalled him. Three failed attempts to login with Jameson's likely username and common, simple passwords timed out his IP address for ten minutes.

Albert spent a while surfing the gray net, chatting up shady characters with handles like 'Rain Dog' and 'Schwarzritter' before he found what he needed. He bought time on a botnet from a cracker called 'Supervato,' and fired it up. The clock ticked while bot-ridden enslaved computers sent a steady stream of login requests to Mizukami and Choudhary's server from IP addresses around the world.

Albert took off his glasses, rubbed his eyes. Kalyani Krishnamurthi sang a torch song over the audio stream. The botnet could hit it lucky any minute, or could take days to brute-force every possible password combination.

No harm leaving the botnet running, even if sensitive data at Mizukami and Choudhary could be cracked by old-fashioned means.


Around nine the following night, Albert wheeled a cleaning cart to Jameson's corner office. He wore faded jeans, earphones piping in Tejano music—accordions and a man crooning about *mi corazon*—and a blue smock with "Jésus – Garcia Sanitation" on the nametag. Two benjamins to the shift foreman had gotten Albert his disguise. He turned on the motion sensors he had clipped to the outside of the trash bag hanging from the cart. In his ear, beeps sounded over the music when he circled the cart on his way into the office.

Jameson had left the lights on. Apparently he was old-school enough to prefer paper. Piles of trifold folders, legal-sized and the color of unfinished pine, lay on the cherry desktop, their twins mirrored in the picture windows. Volumes of patent procedure and regulatory law stood in the bookcase. The computer screen was dark, but a green light glowed on the monitor. Albert picked up the trashcans and walked toward the door. Beeps rang in his ears. He dumped the trashcans' contents into the bag on his cart, then glanced up. A plump woman in a blue smock, fifty feet down the hall, pushed a cleaning cart away from him and toward the elevator lobby. Albert dismounted his vacuum cleaner from the cart and reentered the office.

Most people assumed security threats came from cyberspace, and paid semicompetent hackers to defend their web pages and servers. Yet those same people would leave their password on a notepad in their desks—

He pulled on rubber gloves and pushed the vacuum with one hand while the other opened the drawers. Hanging files; an organizer tray with pens, a ruler, a pad of sticky notes—

Blank. Top sheet, second sheet, last sheet, bottom. Albert set the pad back in place. A thought hit him. He lifted the tray, and for a moment forgot to push the vacuum.

A torn piece of paper held a twelve character string of letters, numbers, and symbols. That was the second most interesting thing in the drawer. A photo of a woman stared up at him. She looked to be in her late twenties, sitting on her ankles and cupping a handful of blond hair over her ear. She wore a coquettish grin and a lacy scarlet ensemble out of a fetishist's dream: bra, panties, stockings, garter. At the bottom, overlaid yellow digits said 03-03-37, over a month before Patricia Jameson's suicide. Albert fished his phone from his pocket and recorded both the photograph and the twelve character string, then put the tray back in place and shut the drawer.

It wasn't Patricia Jameson in the photo, for damn sure. A program could match a name to the face, and whatever the name, it wasn't going to belong to a casual acquaintance. If AffEctive's lawyers could stack a jury with women, Jameson would be in trouble. With luck, Jameson would settle on favorable terms. It took a few seconds for Albert to realize he'd pushed the vacuum over a patch of carpet for the eighth time.

A great night, and it might get even better. He let the vacuum stand alone, roaring, and crossed to Jameson's computer. The CPU's power was on. Albert nudged the mouse, and a login screen dawned on the screen. The username was already filled in.

Albert typed in the password. Moments later, Jameson's desktop appeared.

Albert dug in his pocket for a flash drive, ready to attach it to the computer. Where to start looking for sensitive files? God knew what was on the M&C system, but hopefully Jameson would hide his skeletons on his own hard drive and not the firm's server—

His earphones beeped, again, again. Someone walked down the hall. Oh shit. Maybe someone going into another office? The beeps continued. Albert took a step away from the computer, then realized the monitor still showed Jameson's desktop. Dammit! Turn it off and hope Jameson wouldn't notice. Albert's gloved finger poked the power button, and the monitor blackened. Albert scampered to the vacuum.

Be what he expected. Albert pushed the vacuum and bobbed his head to the music. His heart thudded, and his mouth tasted dry. Chill. Then he realized his rubber gloves were still on.

Jameson's reflection appeared in the window. He had tousled blond hair and craggy cheeks, and a gold pin lifted the knot of his tie away from the placket of his shirt. He crossed to the desk, searched through a stack of folders, took a handful, and left. Not a word to Albert. Not even a glance.

Albert breathed deeply for a few moments. Jameson had better not have forgotten something else. He returned to the computer, slid in the flash drive, and copied over as much of Jameson's hard drive as would fit.

Albert got home around one, and plugged the phone and the flash drive into his computer. He opened FaceInTheCrowd and had it search for matches to the woman in the photograph. He tried Houston first; wouldn't take but a few minutes. Albert started the run and backgrounded it, then gave Patterner the harder job of analyzing the files from Jameson's hard drive. All chaff, probably, but it had to be done.

Go to bed? He could read the name of Jameson's mistress in the morning, but he felt too keyed up. He went to the fridge and cracked open a Soweto Stout. A random preview from the cable company's server showed clips from the Tigres-Pumas Mexican soccer match, tomorrow's Nikkei ticker, and Melissa Tungsiripat's Thai food show *There Once Was a Chef from Near Phuket*. He settled on the soccer match and sipped his beer.

The computer bonged. Albert shut the TV off and entered the den. Onscreen, the blonde appeared in a driver's license photo, pendulous shadows hanging beneath her ears. Lori Schleiermacher, address in a zone of yupscale townhouses between Binz and Southmore, her age twenty-six, an organ donor.

Albert opened another instance of Patterner, this one wgetting on-line search results to find connections between her and Jameson. He turned off the monitor and sat for a moment in the darkened room, cold air tumbling out the vent, his toes scratching the coiled nap of the carpet. Another beer? Why, so he could feel hungover in the morning? Instead he climbed into bed and stared at the ceiling until his eyelids finally drooped.

pfbreak

By the next morning, Patterner had bound Schleiermacher to Jameson. They had met at a health club a year and a half before, and in that time had averaged three phone calls a week between her townhouse and his office. Her debit card had purchased two glasses of wine during an opera intermission; Jameson's had purchased two tickets for the performance. In January, two days before Jameson's birthday, she bought a titanium putter, but she had never golfed.

Albert daydreamed of her testimony. Jameson loathed his wife, had planned divorce for months before her suicide. Albert typed notes, when the phone rang. Who was calling so early? Wait, it was nearly eleven. He picked up.

"Mr. Jimenez?"

"Ms. Nguyen, hello. How may I help you?"

"We wanted to see how you were doing."

"Pretty good." He smiled and said, "Jameson's had a mistress for over a year."

Nguyen huffed out a breath. "Really?"

"Yeah."

"That helps our case. What do we know about her?"

"Mostly name and address at this point. I'm still reeling stuff in.

I'll prepare a report on her within the next couple days."

"I'm looking forward to it," Nguyen said. "We show him up as an adulterer and no jury will buy damages for emotional distress, at least. Our lawyers will love this. Anything else?"

"Not yet, but let's see—" He dragged and clicked until the Patterner window popped up. Though he couldn't mention the source of the files, he could inform Nguyen of the Patterner run's results. He scrolled. "Here's some names. His wife Patricia, Lori Schleiermacher—the mistress—Carter White—some damn attorney—Richard Wang, Steffani Lockhart—"

"Wait. Richard Wang?"

"W-A-N-G. Know him?"

"We have a Richard Wang on our staff," she said.

"Is he an attorney?"

Nguyen said slowly, "He's a tech."

"Was he involved in signing Patricia Jameson up for the trial?"

"No! I mean, no, that's not his job. He's a tech.—Why was he talking to Jameson?"

"I don't have that. Yet. I'll call you back."

"I want to hear as soon as you find out something on Jameson and Wang," she said. "Day or night. I'm serious, don't delay a second. I have to go." A dial tone buzzed in Albert's ear. After a second he cradled the handset.

Nguyen was spooked by Wang's involvement. Why? He called up the files of Jameson's that mentioned Wang and began to read.


Jameson's notes about Wang sounded cryptic—"RW preps" (what did Richard Wang prepare?), and fragments of names that turned out to belong to banks in the Caymans and Slovenia. Albert ran Supervato's icebreaker on the banks, the phone companies, and the credit bureaus, to glean data to link Jameson and Wang. When he checked back a few hours later, blood rushed in his ears as he clicked through the documents.

He picked up the phone, spoke as soon as Nguyen said hello. "Jameson and Wang talked by phone about a dozen times between last October and the week after Patricia Jameson's suicide."

Nguyen took a moment to reply. "We signed people up for the trials in October. Implantation happened early November."

"Jameson also paid Wang."

"I want to know, and I don't want to know. How much?"

"Five and a half million, two last October and the balance after the suicide," Albert said. Nguyen's silence, and the look on her face, hinted at the answer to his next question. "What did Wang do?"

"He was in charge of the assembly of AffEctor units for our trial. He oversaw the workers, and he also did QC on the *E. coli* strains we used. As well as the ones we didn't use. Shit!"

"That sounds serious?"

Her expression showed she realized she'd talked over his head. "In our freezers, we've got stocks of a bunch of strains. Most are low- or non-expressors of serotonin or endorphins or both. In place of our efficacious strain, he could've implanted into the unit substituted another one, say to up serotonin a little and depress endorphins all to hell. That's a combo that can lead to suicide. Wang could've done that and no one else would've known."

"They killed Patricia Jameson," Albert said. As surely as if they'd poisoned her. He remembered what Maria had said and shivered. Damn, it was frightening, to monkey with things that made us human.

"We're talking about more than settling out of court, aren't we?" Nguyen asked.

"We have to call HPD."

Nguyen sniffed out a breath. "Do it. I want these bastards nailed to the wall."


Four days later, Albert waited for Maria at the bar of a business casual restaurant on 290 near her subdivision. Outside, through the horizontal slats of the blinds, traffic crawled outbound on the freeway. Albert sipped his beer, under a faux-distressed farm-road sign and TVs tuned to soccer and baseball. Halfway through his glass, Maria shuffled in. He waved, and she weakly smiled.

After the hellos and the placing of her order, he asked, "What's the scoop?"

"This case is breaking my heart."

"Tell me."

The waitress came over with Maria's daiquiri. "Jameson and Wang are guilty as sin, but we can't get them to trial."

"Shit." Albert stared at his beer and shook his head. "I know my evidence was a little shaky—"

"The judge gave us arrest and search warrants. That's when things fell apart."

"How?"

"During the interrogation Jameson's lawyer quoted the damn statutes at us. 'The Texas Penal Code,'" she said in a poor imitation of an East Texas drawl, "'defines murder as intentionally or knowingly causing the death of an individual.'"

"But—" Jameson didn't shove the pills down his wife's throat. Encouraging formation of a mental state wasn't the cause of death. "No, wait, there's another clause, about intent to cause serious bodily injury and committing an act dangerous to human life—"

"I worked a week of late nights with an assistant DA. I had to leave Eddie with my half-sister, the tatted tramp. Murder, manslaughter, criminally-negligent homicide—the assistant DA told us Jameson's lawyer would get all disputational about what all the words mean. He did."

"What about aiding suicide?"

"Jameson didn't attempt to aid her suicide attempt. He didn't put the pills in her hand."

Albert shook his head. There must have been something to charge him with. "The *AffEctor* unit! Tampering with a consumer product!"

"Maybe," Maria said. "Problem there is it's only a felony to tamper with a product such that that product will probably cause bodily injury or death. But the unit didn't cause her death, did it? That double handful of pills she swallowed is what did."

Albert stared at his beer. "Shit."

"Let alone that we don't have any proof," Maria said. "After the autopsy, guess who the unit got returned to."

"*AffEc*tive?" Maria glumly sucked on her daiquiri straw. "Worse than that."

"Attention Richard Wang." Albert couldn't say another word.

"But even if we could prove it," Maria said, "what've we got? Here's what the assistant DA said. If people are responsible for their actions, then the victim's suicide was entirely her choice, and Jameson walks. And if she wasn't responsible for her suicide, just a puppet of brain chemicals, then Jameson was a puppet of his brain chemicals when he engineered the whole scheme, and he'd hire every big name psychologist to come in and testify that personal responsibility is a myth. These days, Jameson would probably win that too."

"Jesus." But it fit. The inexorable conclusion of the Prozac generation: the will was not free. Either Jameson's hands were clean, or they were robotic tools programmed by brain chemicals. Albert drank, his hand trembling around the handle of the mug. He slammed the mug to the table, and eyed the green and white stained glass of the doors leading to the foyer. Could a robot fling the mug through the window? He shut his eyes and hung his head for a moment. "So what happened?"

"The assistant DA went to her boss, and came back to tell us they wouldn't prosecute. Wang flew to Singapore this morning and is never coming back."

"And Jameson's walking around with millions, courtesy of his dead wife." Poor little rich girl? How was that again? Albert looked at the tabletop, and raised a hand to mask his face.

Maria sucked up the last of her daiquiri. She frowned, then rested her hand on his. "Albert, I, I feel like a fool and I know it, but do you have plans for tonight? I could take a pizza home for us and Eddie, then get him into bed by nine."

"Maria—"

"I'm not talking about something long-term. I know it wouldn't work. Just tonight."

"I...." Why hesitate? So she had belly fat and a son who'd wonder about the noises coming from behind the wall. At his age and erratic position on the middle-class treadmill, a meaningless hookup with a woman like Maria was about the best Albert could get. Better than going home alone to down a six-pack and watch Super Bowl XXXII on ESPN Classic.

But not as good as connecting with someone, anyone, on a level more affirming than a five-minute slap of bodies. Even if they were puppets of brain chemicals, they could both act as if they had agency.

Albert's face firmed and his voice deepened. "Take home the pizza for us and your son. I'm not looking for emotionless sex. After Eddie goes to bed, we'll talk like two people with free will."

# About the Author

Raymund Eich files patent applications, earned a Ph.D., won a national quiz bowl championship, writes science fiction and fantasy, and affirms Robert Heinlein's dictum that specialization is for insects. In a typical day, he may talk with biochemists, electrical engineers, patent attorneys, epileptologists, and rocket scientists. Hundreds of papers cite his graduate research on the reactions of nitric oxide with heme proteins.

Connect with the author at **www.raymundeich.com** or scan the QR code below.

Sign up for his mailing list to receive exclusive, pre-release content about his upcoming books. Your email address will never be shared and you can unsubscribe at any time. Go to **www.raymundeich.com/mailing-list** or scan the QR code below.

# Other Books by the Author

Available wherever books are sold.

Learn more about these titles at our website, **www.cv2books.com**, or scan the QR code below.

# Stone Chalmers

Earth barely survived the 21st Century. Biotechnological and nuclear terrorism, civil war, famine, and ethnic cleansing killed billions. Thousands fled on warpdrive ships to colonize planets around distant suns.

In the 22nd century, after the United Nations established control over Earth, it opened wormhole links to the distant colonies, to prevent a repeat of the previous century's chaos on a galactic scale.

Enter operative Stone Chalmers. Spy. Assassin. Instrument maintaining the UN's order on the settled galaxy.

Opposing him are hostile forces on colony worlds... and within the UN itself.

When Stone clashes with those forces, the UN—and every human world—will be transformed forever.

Learn more about the Stone Chalmers series at **www.cv2books.com/stone-chalmers**, or scan the QR code below.

### The Progress of Mankind (#1)

To maintain order in the 22nd century, the UN relocates undesirables through artificial wormholes onto colony planets. Everyone benefits… except the planets' original colonists.

Now, the newly rediscovered colony of New Moravia learns the UN's plan and fights back.

### The Greater Glory of God (#2)

Thousands fled the chaos of the 21st century on rogue warpdrive ships to settle colony planets. When Earth reunified in the 22nd, its fleets rediscovered the colonies and hunted down the warpdrive ships.

Every warpdrive ship but one.

## To All High Emprise Consecrated (#3)

After unifying Earth, the UN has rediscovered the colony of Minerva. Prosperous and technologically advanced, Minerva quickly submits to UN supremacy.

Surprisingly quickly…

## In Public Convocation Assembled (#4)

After unifying Earth, the UN controls all human colonies scattered through the galaxy by means of wormholes, warpdrive ships, and ruthless operatives. Operatives working to strengthen the UN.

Or destroy it.

## *The Confederated Worlds*

*The purpose of all other combat arms is to put the infantryman in sole possession of the battlefield.*

A thousand years from now, while Earth sleeps in virtual reality, three polities—the Confederated Worlds, the Unity, and the Progressive Republic—strive to connect the scattered, terraformed worlds of humankind by artificial wormholes. When they meet, they clash, in a decades-long struggle of arms that will embroil every human world, in which dedication to duty liberates worlds—and oneself.

Learn more about the Confederated Worlds series at **www.cv2books.com/the-confederated-worlds**, or scan the QR code below.

### *Take the Shilling (Book 1)*

The Confederated Worlds implanted in his brain the skills to make him a soldier. Tomas Neumann had to learn for himself how to survive interstellar war.

### *Operation Iago (Book 2)*

The Confederated Worlds lost the war. Can Lt. Tomas Neumann win the peace against elusive, deceptive foes out to turn the Confederated Worlds against itself?

### *A Bodyguard of Lies (Book 3)*

Assigned to the halls of power, only Capt. Tomas Neumann can save the Confederated Worlds from the ultimate treachery.

# Novels

## The Blank Slate

Neuroscience entrepreneur Clay Shieffer must stop a tyrannical president... because he unwittingly gave the tyrant power over the human mind.

## New California

After New California's founder committed suicide, two men vied to rule the colony.

Ashwin George, supported by the colony's elite and the Chinese company dominating half the settled galaxy.

Against him, Desmond Park, nanotechnology engineer, armed with the most formidable weapon of all.

A single idea.

## The Reincarnation Run

Skeptical spacejock Landry Krieger knows exactly how to smuggle the "reborn" spiritual leader of an oppressed people past their conquerors... but the boy's priests—and governess—shake up his orderly plans.

# Short Novels

## The ALECS Quartet

*He had a month to learn the planet's mysteries—and Juliette's.*

His cover story: return to Elard to dismantle his sect's missionary work to the planet's natives.

His true mission: investigate decades-old mysteries of love and death.

His objective: return to Earth with his discovery.

If he can.

## A Mighty Fortress

Theodore and his team from the Lutheran Interstellar Terraforming Society would transform a barren, rocky world into a refuge of faith and life.

Or die trying.

# Collections

## The First Voyages: The Complete Science Fiction Stories 1998-2012

From 21st century asteroid settlements to World War II Romania, from an Earth dominated by immortal aliens to Christ's empty tomb, a fresh, distinctive voice in science fiction will take you on journeys to the photosphere of the sun, the coding regions of DNA, and the complexities of the human psyche.

## Stage Separations: The Complete Science Fiction Stories 2013-2018

In these pages, you can...

...race against time to solve mysteries hidden in a planet's vast desert—and in a woman's heart ...learn the true story of a president's assassination ...journey 14,000 miles to a high-tech fountain of youth ...win or go "home"—to an Earth you've never seen

and explore six other worlds created by a distinctive voice in twenty-first century science fiction.